A Pillar of Fire

Casey Curry

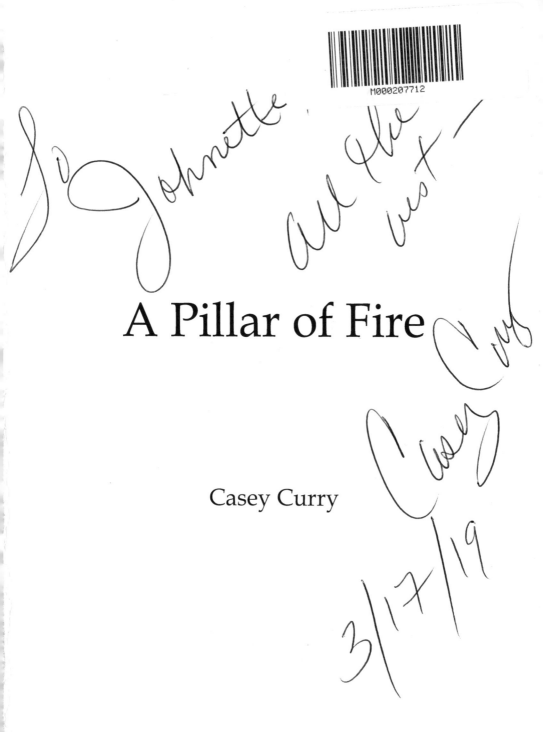

To Johnette,
all the best —

Casey Curry

3/17/19

ISBN-13: 978-0578412467

ISBN-10: 0578412462

DEDICATION

This book is dedicated to those who wait patiently at God's door through the darkest of nights. To the outliers everywhere, the falsely imprisoned and falsely accused, the abused, attacked, the maligned, misunderstood and all who suffer in silence. To those led by a pillar of fire out of the wilderness. This is for you.

Weeping may endure for a night but joy comes in the morning.

Perfection is not attainable, but if we chase perfection
we may catch excellence.

ACKNOWLEDGMENTS

This book would not exist without the push of my many devoted readers and the pull of book clubs all over the country. To all of my readers and fans, your investment in Ella Jean and Pam and the cast of characters energizes me and confirms that there is indeed an appetite for "other" stories.

I couldn't have come to the last word on the last page without the support and expertise of the editorial staff at Ellarose Publishing, especially Ms. Walker. I acknowledge your support and undergirding.

I thank my three living, beautiful "daughter friends" for their encouragement and support of this book. Bruce, I am forever grateful for you being a load-bearing wall and for your infinite kindness and patience.
To my beloved fourth daughter, my baby, Tori Rose who inspires me from a far, waiting patiently at heaven's gate, I am grateful that love never dies.

Finally, God's grace pressed me forward to create time for my craft and to believe that joy would come "…in the morning"

In the beginning was the word...

PROLOGUE

Time is a strange concept. It can be very real and then not exist at all. However, I am dead so none of it matters.

I can't believe I'm dead. I am happier than I have ever been and I am considered by most to be dead. Who knew that life for us would really begin, once that last breath was taken? The hardest thing for me to get use to in this amazing new life is weightlessness and the way time passes, or doesn't. There is an utterly unexplainable contentment. I wish all could experience it. Unfortunately, not everyone chooses a path that leads him or her here. I often think of my wife who departed this earth years before I did. I do not feel sad because sorrow is an emotion no longer on my registry of emotions but I do wish for different outcomes. Jean is miserable and being able to witness her torture and pain brings me no pleasure. There is an ugliness to every minute of her existence in eternity. I can see her in the sunken place she exists in as I glance there without effort from time to time. She knows I am watching and that adds to her misery. Her regret, along with that of our granddaughter, Michelle and many of my friends, brings me no joy. Nevertheless, it is real.

I know things. Period. That is the other thing that is strange about being dead or should I say this new endless life. I now understand why it was my destiny to fall in love with a woman too free with her body and too familiar with hard liquor and have a child with her. The scorn I endured on earth was nothing compared to the joy I got from those two girls. It was predestined that I, Jonas Ezra Sloane become their "Daddy Sloane", the father Ella Jean never had and the example Pam would use to measure men for the rest of her life. It was the fulfillment of past prayers and ancient plans, far beyond me. I know that now, as I know everything, no longer seeing through a glass darkly. The memories of the past are softened yet crystal clear, as are both the present and the future.

I see things. I know things. I remember many things, all things. Now I will share with you all that I know because I know you are curious and seek answers. You seek answers that only time or the absence of time can provide. I have loved and watched over them all. I have interceded on spiritual levels, unknown to many, on their behalf. But I have never interfered. For I am powerless to shape destiny.

The Past

Therefore, we are always confident, knowing that, while we are at home in the body, we are absent from the Lord: [7] For we walk by faith, not by sight.[8] We are confident… and willing rather to be absent from the body, and to be present with the Lord.[9] Wherefore we labor, that, whether present or absent, we may be accepted of him.

Corinthians 5: 6-9

1

The day I met Jean the sun was perched high in the sky. It was scorching hot and the iced tea was exceptionally cold. The iceman delivered two huge blocks of ice to the church picnic and five soft round women in thin cotton pressed and starched dresses stood chipping away at the huge blocks with ice picks while a tall thin woman wearing a white blouse and a grey plaid skirt stirred a huge basin of tea. The joy in their laughter and familiarity with each other drew me in their direction. Everything about them was inviting. There were about seventy people on the church lawn that day at the annual St. Mark AME church picnic, sponsored by the Lay organization. I wish I could remember the exact date but I cannot. Time and the idea of dates, months and years are erased from my mind forever. I just know, past, present and future and all details exist within those perimeters.

And there she was. She was the most beautiful woman I had ever seen. Soft black curls fell on her shoulders and she was laughing. Her laughter was loud and pure and her red full lips were wide open. An immediate desire washed over me, a need to touch her caramel face and kiss her ripe red lips. At once, I felt an urge of shame and almost embarrassment. I was and remain a man of faith and discipline and women had never been a stumbling block for me. This was new and strange, uncomfortable. I took a few ladies out here and there, but I had never been married and was not looking to join up with no readymade family either. The yellow cotton dress she was wearing had ruffles along the neckline and the exposed flesh along her neck, arm and legs glistened. She wiped at her neck and the entrance of her ample cleavage with a handkerchief she pulled from her dress pocket. Asking one of the brothers, I would later find out her name was Jean and she had a little girl.

The first time I saw my wife Jean's baby, I knew she was lacking love. That little Ella Jean was as smart as a whip and was like a little broken bird when I first started taking up with her mother. The way she flinched every time her mother moved her hand and never asked for help with anything told me two things. First, she knew that hand to be the source of danger and pain rather than love and comfort. Jean had been slapping and hitting the child. Secondly, I could tell that she had not been mothered and had resigned herself at the tender age of four that she had only herself to rely on. It was the strangest thing to wake up to a child her age on a stool in the kitchen washing dishes or tending to a pot her mother had left on the stove before passing out drunk on the couch.

Because I refused to spend the night or sleep with her until after we were married, I didn't see the details of the ugliness until it was too late. But even if I had seen it, had known it, I now know it wouldn't have mattered. I was supposed to marry her and love that baby. I was supposed to be the one to give that baby a sister to love, someone that would return that love. When my only daughter Pamela was born my life felt complete. Caring for the three of them became my mission and my ministry. I have since learned that you don't always get to choose your crops. More often than not, they are pre-planted and your job is to tend to the fields and harvest the yield. That is what I did, until the day I died.

Not one to be shy around women, I was taken aback at the feelings of excitement and nervous energy that came over me as I approached the group of ladies, penetrating their sacred circle of sisterhood. They stood quietly watching me as I drew closer, filled with all the usual small town curiosity about outsiders.

"Good afternoon ladies, how's everybody today?"

My eyes were fixed only on Jean as I greeted them all.

Smiles and nods were returned and I extended my hand to the woman in the yellow dress.

"Allow me to introduce myself; I don't believe we've met. I'm Jonas Sloane from over in Yazoo County but everybody calls me Joe. Years ago, my mama and daddy were members of this church. They are buried in the cemetery over there. I come back when I can to the annual picnic... and you are?"

I tipped my straw hat and extended my hand, feeling quite foolish. I don't know why I told her all that stuff about my ma and pa. But I stood staring and waited for her to speak.

"Jean Washington, nice to meet you." Placing a soft slender hand in mine, she smiled and squeezed my hand quickly before letting go.

To my disappointment, she was wearing a thin gold band on the ring finger on her left hand. The lady was married. She walked away to tend to a group of children playing with a ball nearby. I did not know it then but one of them was her little girl, Ella Jean. She was three years old and they were both all smiles.

I ate the BBQ ribs, roasted pork, the fried chicken cooked in the big black kettle full of grease atop the raging fire, and the potato salad sitting in the tub of ice dished out by the women who smelled like fresh baked sweet potato pies. I ate and I ate some more. Washing it all down with a mason jar full of homemade sweet tea complete with lemon slices and seeds. It was like liquid sunshine. My eyes were fixed on the woman, Jean in the yellow dress, captivated by her easy smile and slender body. Busy slicing pound cakes, tall coconut layer cakes, and sweet potato and lemon meringue pies, she was impervious to my penetrating gaze. Jean was working the dessert table and that's where she belonged. It suited her fine. After handing me a generous slice of potato pie, she never acknowledged my presence again that day.

2

The sun was setting and men were wrapping up games of horseshoes and checkers as the women scraped the scraps from the plates into the compost pen and placed them into the washbasin filled with soapy water. The children were beginning to show signs of fatigue as the annual day of fellowship came to a close. I made my way to the small well kempt cemetery on the far corner of the church grounds to pay my respects to my ma and daddy. They would later tell me when we met in eternity that they saw the significance of that day from afar. I was supposed to be in that graveyard on that day at that time. It was my destiny.

The modest headstones and crosses stood in neat, proud rows on the bed of thick green grass, blanketing the dead bodies beneath the earth. I passed several uncles and Robbie Ray, my cousin who drowned at seven playing in the Chickasawhay River. I don't think uncle Henry ever got over his boy's death. Finally, I came to the resting place of my parents, side by side. I opened my mouth to say something, but before I could greet my dearly departed parents, I was startled by moaning and rustling sounds. Not here. I remember thinking, everyone needs to be dead here.

Looking around, I tried to trace the moaning sounds and pinpoint the direction. Near the caretaker's very modest house to the right of the parsonage, the disruption became louder.

It was her, Jean. She was pushing him with her free hand, desperately trying to move her mouth away from his. The man, a very large yellow-skinned man, had the woman pinned against a massive oak tree under a canopy of hanging moss that seemed to enhance the ugliness of the scene. His right hand was on his zipper and his left arm pinned the woman against the tree while he held the soft folds of fabric of her yellow dress bunched to her waist.

It all happened so quickly. The blow from the tree limb startled him and he fell forward, slumped at the base of the tree. Out cold. The woman whimpered, pulling her dress down and smoothing her hair that had become wild and crazy. It matched her expression. Jean fixed her eyes on me for just a moment that day with a mixture of anger, disgust and gratitude, while fixing the front of her dress. She promptly turned and stomped out of the cemetery. No words were uttered. I stood there not knowing what to do. Placing the stick down next to the man, I checked to make sure he was breathing. Hesitating before heading back to my parents' gravesite just for a moment, staring at the big man slumped over on his side at my feet. He looked to be sleeping, worry free. Did she know him? Should I call the police? Did I witness a crime? Should I try to find her and see if she was okay or mind my business? Not sure what to do, I did nothing. I did not want this woman to think I was chasing her and I didn't want to be the knight in shining armor. It wasn't my way. I had done enough already. But it was the right thing to do. A man ought not to behave that way with a woman, any woman. It just wasn't right.

I left the cemetery that day without so much as a word to ma and pa. My usual moments of reflection and memories with my parents fell silent. I had nothing to say because my mind was a jumble of thoughts and questions about what I had just seen and done. I took my leave.

As I made my way past the neat graves, the air fragrant with the smell of moss and clover, new questions clouded my thinking. Jean had run ahead of me, as I stood there motionless. I thought long and hard about the woman and the big man and pondered my many unanswered questions. A horrible wind blew up and it began to rain. The light rain felt good on the back and shoulders of my white dress shirt as I traveled on the neat path and through the open gate of the cemetery. It was supposed to be a place of peace. Today it was anything but. The rain came down in a steady rhythm.

It was dark now and the crowd was gone. Two or three people gathered remnants of the earlier festivities. They moved in a choreographed silence returning the church grounds to its serene and empty state and the folding tables, chairs, platters and bowls to their places.

I thought about all that had taken place. I wondered about this woman I'd just met, wanted to see her and make sure she was all right. From that day on until the day I left this earth, I never stopped protecting the lady in the yellow dress.

3

The rain was coming down pretty steadily as I climbed into the cab of my old Chevy truck and put the key into the ignition in one swift effort. The truck was about ten years old, but it was clean and reliable and paid for. I never believed in having a lot of bills, payments, debts and I didn't need a lot of stuff. The engine hummed down the main highway leading out of town as the sky grew dark. I needed to know more and I knew where I had to go.

Veering off the interstate, I took a left turn onto a dirt road, marked only by a series of worn mailboxes and an empty produce stand. It was dark and I hoped to remember which house was my uncle Isaac's amid the ten or so houses that peppered the road. Some of the lights inside of the homes were on as families went on with their Saturday evening routines. I was about to show up unannounced to inquire about a woman. This was totally out of character. That is often the way life on Earth is.

My uncle Isaac passed away years ago and left his house to his oldest son, Isaac Jr. as his inheritance. I pulled up to the neat little house perched on cinder blocks. The yellow porch light was on, my cousin stood up from his rocking chair in an act of propriety as my car approached his house, and I turned off the engine. His dog, Butch stood too. It was as if they both wondered who I was and what I wanted. Recognizing the truck, Isaac came to the edge of the porch and hollered, "Hey Jonas, that you man?"

Running up to the screened-in porch to escape the rain, I hugged the short brown portly man with the huge smile and kind eyes.

"Yeah man, it's me. Came down to the church picnic and thought I'd stop by and see you before heading out of town." I lied.

"Good. Good. Come on in, Patsy is inside, she be happy to see you!"

The house was small and the front room was filled with a weathered gold colored couch, a coffee table and two brown chairs. There were plants everywhere. I quickly sat down on the couch across from my cousin. This was long before cell phones and before you had to have an invitation or appointment to visit someone. We were simple, country folk and hospitality was a gift extended generously.

The house smelled good and felt warm. Patsy, my cousin's wife and high school sweetheart, appeared from behind a squeaky door. She was a deep brown thin woman with a broad smile and wavy hair piled high atop her head held together with a faded scarf. Wearing a simple tan housedress, she smiled coming towards me.

"Hey Jonas, what wind blew you in here?"

Her hug was pure. It was warm and gentle and she made me feel like I was welcomed there. They were family. That meant something then, even though it had been years since I'd seen them, time stood still. I had so many questions and I didn't know how to start or where to start. Clearing my throat, I began with some small talk that made absolutely no sense.

"This rain is coming down pretty hard now. Have y'all had a lot of rain this season...How the kids doing? Do they get home often?"

I blurted out nonsense in rapid fire as Patsy and Isaac just sat half in amusement and half in wonder. They shared softly, that this was the rainy season and something about the squash and beans in the garden really doing well and tomatoes growing. Moving on to my next area of inquiry, Patsy quietly left the room to retrieve three black and white photographs of their son and daughter and their families, the girl and her husband lived in Chicago and their son, Isaac III, lived in Rocky Mount, North Carolina with his wife and two boys. They said they saw the kids a couple of times a year and everybody was just fine. Then there was an uncomfortable silence, broken by Patsy asking if I wanted something to drink, tea, water, whiskey?

I passed on the libations and thought I had better get to the point.

"So I met a woman today out at the church picnic. Her name was Jean and she had a little girl, is she from around here?" I finally got to the point and sounded like a plum fool. Isaac chuckled and Patsy looked straight ahead, out the window as if willing herself not to speak. My cousin told me that the woman was new in town, had been around for about a year. She'd come with a man that disappeared. Some say he ran off with another woman, some say he got locked up or worse. But she lived alone over cross the railroad tracks and trouble seemed to follow her.

I wanted to know what kind of trouble, but before I could fix my mouth to ask, Patsy spoke up with a firmness that denied her soft persona.

"Jonas, Jean is a pretty woman, which you saw for yourself today, but she drinks and likes fun a little too much. Men flock to her like flies to molasses and they is always fighting and mess going on wherever she is. I don't think she be suitable for you at all. She don't seem much like your type. I'm just saying."

I nodded and tried to look concerned. But I wasn't at all, wasn't deterred in the least bit. When something is your destiny, it is your destiny and sometimes all the warnings, logic and better judgement in the world will mean nothing. This was one of those times. We made a little more small talk about family members, catching up on births, deaths, unions and illnesses. I said my goodbyes and headed back home. The rain had stopped.

4

Within six months, I had relocated back home and bought a little house. I set up my house painting business and picked up a few customers that needed my services. I started going to church regularly. Not so much to see Jean, but just because it was the right thing to do. It was my custom and it pleased the father. That is taken right from the bible. It is recorded in one of the gospels as the reason Jesus himself went to the Synagogue. Yeah, because it was his custom and it pleased the father. Those were good enough reasons for me. My faith was not complicated and was never predicated by what somebody else was doing or saying. So I knew that the little "jack legged" preacher was running women and that the head of the Steward Board was sleeping with a woman (choir director) and a man (pianist) in addition to his wife. I went to worship, thank God for my blessings and enjoy the benefits of being a part of a community.

I had seen the big yellow man that I knocked out in the cemetery that day a couple of times and found out his name was Bert. I also know now that he was her husband's best friend. He had lured her into the cemetery that day with the promise of taking a walk to get away from everyone else so he could tell her where her husband, Bittie Boy was and pass along an important word from him. That was a ruse and his reputation as a brute was well known. As I initially thought, he was indeed the worst kind of man. He never saw me that day, so I had no trouble with him on the few occasions our paths crossed in town.

I sat in the back of the church each Sunday on the same side as Jean and her little girl. I was about five rows from them except for the Sundays she ushered. On those Sundays, the baby-sat on the front row with one of the older sisters and Jean stood in the middle of the aisles directing people to their seats and passing out fans with pictures of black families on them. She wore a white thin blouse and a black skirt, nylon hose and flat black shoes. Those were my favorite Sundays. I just drank her up, spending most of the service staring at her and looking forward to the offering when she would lean over me passing the collection plate down my row.

Something inside told me it was time to ask her out and so I made the plan to go beyond my usual small talk about the weather, the sermon and the choir. When church let out, I lingered by my truck parked on the grassy field in front of the church and waited for her to come out. She was one of the last to leave the white clapboard church that day, but I waited patiently. She and the child usually walked home or rode with one of the widows. I remember that it was hot. I think it was late summer but I can't be sure. She was wearing a pink dress with front pockets and short sleeves. On her head, a pink hat hugged her head like a crown or some kind of floral headband. She had on stockings and her usual black flat shoes.

"Good afternoon Jean, how you two doing today?" I spoke calmly and deliberately trying to exude confidence, kindness and good intentions.

"Hey Sloane, we alright. How you doing today?" She smiled and continued to walk towards the road.

"Can I offer you two ladies a ride home? It's awfully hot to be walking today, Miss Jean." Out of nowhere, I winked. Actually winked at this woman. Never done anything like that in my life. Never felt the need. Just wasn't my way. I have no idea what came over me and had me actin' like a backwoods Don Juan. She smiled and said okay. I moved slowly to the passenger side of my truck and opened the door. I lifted Ella Jean into the cab of my truck and helped Jean in next. Her arm felt soft and warm. It was the softest thing I had ever touched. No lie.

On the way home, we didn't talk much. She gave directions to her house and I drove. The little girl hummed and played with a small pebble she had in her hand. I stopped the car in front of a small row of shabby rental houses. Jean thanked me for the ride and asked if I wanted to come inside. I agreed to come in for just a little bit. Her house was an open book and consisted of four white rooms. There was a small front room with a brown plaid couch, a scarred up end table and a gold colored lamp and a coffee table. There was a kitchen with a rickety table with three chairs in front of the stove, a small bathroom with a claw foot tub and finally, a bedroom with one large bed, a dresser and a Jenny Lind style crib. Everything was neat but nothing was bright, glorious or spectacular. The furniture looked like it came with the place. Nothing in the house said a young mother and daughter lived there. It was a modest home but there was something very sad and lonely about it.

She explained she didn't have any food cooked yet but she offered me a choice, some lemonade or some whiskey. I chose the lemonade. She poured herself a class of whiskey from a cabinet under the sink and me a glass of lemonade from a pitcher in her near empty icebox. The little girl, Ella Jean, disappeared into the bedroom as Jean closed the bedroom door. That bothered me, so I got up and opened the door to find the little girl perched in the corner holding and talking quietly to a worn cloth doll. The curtains were drawn and the room was dark. She didn't seem sad, nor did she appear happy. It was odd but it was as if to be away from her mother was a part of her routine.

"Come back. Why'd you leave us Ella?" I bent down in front of her.

"I'm sposed to." She looked up at me with a blank stare.

I lifted her up, carried her back into the front room, and sat her on the couch between her mother and me. Jean looked surprised, but smiled just a little and didn't utter a word. The baby-sat there as we each drank from our glasses. It was peaceful, a glimpse of the Sunday afternoons ahead. I decided I should leave but wanted to come back the next day and the next day. I asked Jean if she would mind if I called on the two of them. She said that would be okay so I asked if I could come by after work on Monday and told her I would bring dinner. She put her empty glass down on the coffee table and so I did too. I got up and said goodbye to Ella Jean, kissing her on the forehead. She started to get up from the couch, but Jean gave her a sharp look and she scooted back and sat motionless. As the door closed, I wondered what the rest of her evening would hold.

5

I showed up the next day with a bag of groceries and Jean answered the door looking groggy. Placing the bag on the table, I looked around for Ella Jean. The bedroom door was closed. Jean sat down at the kitchen table and propped her head up with her hand, elbow resting on the cool metal tabletop. I unpacked the bag, placing some items in the icebox, others in the cupboard and the ingredients for dinner on the table. In the icebox went a dozen eggs, a slab of bacon in butcher paper and a carton of milk. In the cupboard, I placed a large jar of instant coffee, five pounds of sugar, two pounds of flour, Crisco, 2 cans of peaches, a bag of rice and a can of mackerel fish and Carnation milk. On the table was a whole chicken, three large sweet potatoes and fresh green beans in a paper crate. After everything was in place, I remembered what was in my shirt pocket.

"How was your day and where's the baby?" I pulled out the peppermint stick and looked towards the bedroom. Jean called for the girl and the door opened slowly. She stood in the doorway, she had been crying.

"Hey sweetheart, I have a present for you." She didn't smile but moved quietly towards the extended peppermint.

"Is it ok? Can she have this?" I looked back towards her mother still sitting at the table, eyes focused on something neither the child nor I could see. Jean nodded. I picked Ella Jean up, placed the piece of candy into her small brown hand,

and told her she could eat it after dinner. I wanted to ask her what was wrong. I didn't. I sat her at the kitchen table with her mother. She sat there, clutching the candy and her doll looking down and sniffling.

Of course, now I know. I know that she had been slapped for wetting her pants. Jean had been talking to the yellow man, Bert just an hour before I arrived that day. He had stopped by and she wouldn't let him in the house. When he came to the door, she'd told the little girl to go into the bedroom and not to move. She perched in her corner and did just as she was told. But they talked for a long time; she could hear her mother yelling and the man trying to coax his way into the house. When Jean finally slammed the door yelling at the man "if he ever came by there again she'd call the police"- Ella Jean was standing in the corner wet. Pee dripped down her legs and into her socks and shoes. She was only three years old.

Jean flew into a rage and as is more often the case with these things, it was less about the little girl and more about anger and fear. She was angry that her husband, Bittie Boy, had been gone for almost a year now. She was angry that his piece of trash friend had tried to rape her and was always lying and trying to get to her. She feared she could not take care of her child, she feared she was a bad mother.

I would come to know the whole story in eternity, but on that day, I just chose to light the pilot of her tiny gas stove, rinse the sweet potatoes and put them in an old pie tin. I found salt and pepper, cleaned, and dressed the chicken, rubbing some oil on the skin and placed it in the oven along with the potatoes. Cutting a chunk off the slab of bacon, I tossed it into a pot of boiling water while I cleaned and snipped the tips off the green beans. She didn't have many spices, so I used what she had. I cleaned up as I went along and finally with dinner on, I sat down with the two of them and once again, there was silence. It wasn't a bad silence; in fact, there was a kind of peace to it. It suited me fine.

There were no words. When dinner was finally ready, she got up and started putting food on plates. We sat and Jean looked at me, waiting for what I now know was me to bless the food, or say grace. Three heads bowed and we closed our eyes.

"Father, bless this food for the nourishment of our bodies and bless the hands that prepared it. In Jesus' name, we pray. Amen"

Each of us picked up a fork and began to eat. Little Ella Jean cleaned her plate and asked for seconds on everything. Jean shot her a look of disapproval.

"Let the baby eat," I chided. Her face softened and I refilled the child's plate and sat it in front of her. She looked around the table in wonder and seemed happier than I'd seen her thus far. It doesn't take much to please one who has had so little. I so wanted both of them to be happy and would spend the rest of my life trying desperately to make it so.

6

Jean and I were married three months later in September. Our simple ceremony was in the church my parents had gone to find their peace with God and work out their own soul salvation. Their remains lay unbothered in the church cemetery where I knocked the guy out almost a year ago to the day for trying to have his way with my wife. Jean was now my wife and I was happy. I felt my parents somehow approved. This was the way it was supposed to be. It was predestined in some way and I was not one to believe in a lot of hocus pocus spirituality. I was and remain a simple man with simple needs.

Jean and Ella Jean moved into my house and Ella Jean had her own bedroom for the first time in her life. We got a second hand twin bed and bought a pink and white quilt from one of the ladies at church at the church yard sale. I got pink curtains and sheets from the catalogue at Sears and Roebuck. I made a little pine desk and chair and stained it for her, mounting three shelves on the wall with the extra wood. I figured she would use those for her toys and books, as she got older.

My wife took little interest in any of this. She didn't care in the way that the world tells us mothers should or always do. She just didn't. I think she loved Ella Jean. But she loved her in a way only a broken woman could and to the extent that she knew love. Love for her had been defined in the narrowest of terms long ago and that was how it

s one of two things. Love was sweat and lust,
bbed up against and loving on a man. Love,
_, ..onymous with sex first and foremost.
ɔecondly, it was shouting, praying and crying out to God for
mercy and forgiveness. Love was sex. Love was church.
There was little room and little knowledge of much else in her
life experiences.

Her mother, Adeline, was fourteen when she was born.
Wilson was ending his Presidency and money was tight for
everybody. Illegal stills pumping out bootleg whiskey rested
in the backwoods of the south. This was the new cash crop of
the prohibition era. A lot of money was made and many lives
were lost. Where there is dirty money, illegal activity, there is
always violence. Her father was a pawn in a game he refused
to play. All this I learned after I died.

The whole time we were married, Jean never talked
about herself and got uncomfortable whenever I asked. But I
saw the night her father was killed vividly in the hereafter.
The hymnologist was right. You truly understand it all better
by and by. I wish I'd known it while I was still with her. I
don't think it would have changed what I did or how I treated
her, because I was always good to Jean. But it sure would
have changed how I felt.

7

The night was dark and Adeline and her husband, Elijah had just laid down in their shack of a cabin with the baby next to them in the wooded cradle. They had worked the three acres the same as any day and ate their supper. Sharecropping was the only life they had known and they were happy. Minutes after they snuffed out the kerosene lamp they lay sleeping the good sleep that comes from being loved and a good day's work. Elijah pressed himself against his wife with his hand across her stomach. She lay in her thin cotton gown, soft hair braided in two plaits on her shoulder tied with scraps of fabric and her hand resting on his hand claiming her warm belly.

They didn't hear the horses but they both jumped up when the latch broke, flinging the door wide open. The room was illuminated by fire from torches, gleaming white robes and hoods. Elijah jumped to his feet exposing bare chest and feet, clad only in his pajama pants made from flour sacks sewn together and tied with string at the waist.

"Boy come outcha naw!" The voice roared and he knew his life was over. He knew it was the same voice that had asked him to run moonshine for him too many times. Yesterday, Grady Macklin had asked for what appeared now to be the final time. Baby Jean Ann screamed and Adeline stood clutching her in the corner afraid to cry or speak as four men dragged Elijah out of the two-room house and threw him across a waiting mule. "We gone teach you danight to say naw to a white man, I don't know who you thank you is but we go settle dis heah danight." Elijah looked back at his home, his wife and his child with a look that said many things. It was goodbye, I'm *sorry, I'm helpless and I love you all in a glance with no words. When the light of fire was gone and the dust of horses hoofs had settled, Adeline stood in the corner of her bedroom with the broken front door hanging on its hinge until the sky turned light.*

Jean never knew her father and never knew how much he and her mother loved each other. Their kind of love was foreign to her. Elijah's body was never found and there was never a search for him. That was simply the way it was. Adeline strapped her baby on her back and worked like a mule from sun up until sun down in the fields. After the word got around about Elijah, Joe Smith came by to repair her door and took to coming by to help get her crops and money settled to the man they sharecropped for. He was quiet and basic. She was numb. Broken. Elijah was the beginning of passion, all of nineteen and her thirteen when they took up together. That was buried with him.

Adeline would never love another man but would go on to have eight more children and bury two more husbands. One year after Elijah was taken from their home, she married fifty-five year old Joe Smith, who worked for the blacksmith. She buried him ten years later when she was only twenty-four years old with five additional mouths to feed. At twenty-six, she married a farmer who had his own land and whose wife had died the year before. He was sixty and all of his children were older than his new wife, Adeline. She bore him three sons and worked like a spiritless slave until he died in another woman's bed at age seventy-five.

By the time Adeline was forty-one she was ancient. She had cared for Jean's basic needs but had nothing else to give the child. By the time Jean was five, she was helping her mother care for the new babies who seemed to come every other year as if on some masochistic schedule. This framework shaped my wife. I knew it but she did not; she only knew the misery and the hardship of it, the day-to-day struggle of it.

I also knew that her father, Elijah was lynched that night. Hung high from an oak tree in a clearing designated for such southern traditions. He did not cry, for he knew that a life of running moonshine was a death sentence too. He understood the desperation of his choices and prayed to God to take care of his wife and baby. His last thoughts were thanking God for love, for allowing him to love. They yanked the rope and then lowered his lifeless naked body; they cut his genitals off and put them in his mouth. The six men hooped and hollered, working themselves up into the worst of themselves. Feeling brave and powerful, they sat around and drank moonshine until a little before the sun was to come up and then they gathered kindling wood, twigs and leaves and made a bed for Elijah. The six men set the whole thing on fire and waited until there was little left before putting the fire out. Sharing final greetings, they went home to their wives to get ready for their day jobs as the local sheriff, deputy, the blacksmith, the owner of the general store and his son, Grady. Grady and his father owned a plot of land they pretended to farm. Moonshine was their real business and they meant business.

8

We were moving along at a steady pace when something wonderful happened. At least it was wonderful for me. I hadn't planned it or even asked God for it in my most secret of prayers. Jean was pregnant with my child. We were going to have a baby and Ella Jean would have a little brother or sister. Everything changed for me. I truly felt the Lord was smiling on me and giving me the unspoken desires of my heart.

We continued to go to church and Ella Jean grew plump and more relaxed. Still guarded in her mother's presence, she laughed and talked to me more each day and called me Daddy Sloane. I liked that. I liked it a lot. We sat in the little church, Jean and I, with Ella Jean between us as the choir belted out Blessed Assurance from the choir stand. The wind whipped at the thin windows and they shook. Winter would soon be here to stay and the baby was due in November. We had been married for only six months before she got pregnant. Jean looked tired and didn't seem nearly as happy as I was about the baby and being pregnant. I'd made her promise not to drink. But I know good and well she didn't keep that promise. When Ella Jean and I got home from work and the babysitter's house, my wife, Jean was always knocked out in bed with the curtains drawn and the lights out. She never talked too much about her day and often didn't wake up for dinner. Little Ella Jean and I ate together after she sat at the table and told me all about her day as I cooked each night.

I just prayed that the baby would be healthy and all right.

Jean didn't usher this Sunday. I was startled out of my thoughts by the elderly gentlemen handing the worn collection basket down my row. I placed fifty cents in the basket and passed it along. Ella sat nestled between us, sucking her thumb and stroking the doll hair made of black yarn. The benediction came all too soon and signaled the close of service. As we stood to file out of the church with the other parishioners, I wondered what was in store for our little family. I whispered a silent prayer of safety and protection, a prayer for prosperity, purpose and peace for all of us.

The drive home was quiet and I continued to pray. This time my silent petition to God was that I would have the strength and wisdom to take care of Jean and Ella Jean and the new baby. I did not know anything about raising kids. I'd seen my father's example as a husband and daddy. He was gentle and a provider. He never raised his voice and always treated my mother with respect. I vowed to use his example and the biblical dictate to love my wife as Christ loved the church and gave his life for it.

My wife was a little irritable and restless. She went to bed as soon as we got home from church, closing the door to our bedroom and withdrawing herself from all things family. I promised to bring her something good to eat later and immediately started on dinner after placing my tie and jacket neatly over the back of the couch.

"Can I play in the yard, Daddy Sloane?" Ella Jean asked quietly as if instinctively knowing she needed to get far away and not disturb her mother's rest.

"Yes, baby girl. Don't go outside the gate, hear?'

"Yes sir, I won't.

After changing from the little blue church dress into a gray and yellow-checkered play shirt, overalls and sneakers, she headed out the backdoor to swing on the tire swing I'd hung from the oak tree in the center of the yard.

Alone in the kitchen, I began cleaning the trout Ella Jean and I had caught yesterday and seasoning the cornmeal to batter them. I'd dreamed about the baby again last night. She was beautiful and we named her Pamela, after my aunt. I hoped Jean would go along with that name. It didn't sound like anything she would like but when it came to the baby, she didn't have a lot of opinions or want to make many decisions. So I was guessing Pam would be a fine name for our daughter.

After the last piece of fish was fried, I called Ella Jean into the house to wash her hands for dinner. I had cooked a pot of cabbage last night and made potato salad. I warmed up the cabbage in the big stockpot and put the potato salad bowl in the center of the table. Next to it, I placed a bottle of Texas Pete hot sauce, a small plate of sliced white bread and the butter dish. Ella Jean and I ate our dinner and enjoyed the peaceful little girl chatter that had become her specialty. She talked about singing in the Sunbeam choir at church and asked what a solo was. When I told her it was singing without the other voices, she frowned and told me she hoped she never got one then. I chuckled. She went on giggling, eating her fish, carefully picking out bones and talking about numbers and colors and who could run the fastest of all the kids at the babysitter, Miss Olivia's, house. She was happiest and most relaxed when her mother was not around.

My wife, Jean joined us less and less and I told myself it was because she was in a family way. She was pregnant and tired. Now I suspect there was more to it. As hard as I tried, I don't think I made her happy. I don't think anyone or anything could have. There was a sadness and a longing that Jean Sloan carried until the day she died. Giving her my name, my seed, my love and care and respectability made no difference. I believe she loved me as much as she could love anyone, but I know that the joy in her eyes that was there for a brief time when we first got married was gone. I think she dreaded as much as feared motherhood and all that it would mean with the new baby. She was scared of what was to come and perhaps rightly so.

9

After the kitchen was cleaned and the dishes were washed, dried and put away, I ran a bath for little Ella and laid out her pajamas. She was old enough to bathe herself and brush her teeth. I told her a bedtime story like I did every night. Usually it was a story based on a bible passage, mostly the 23rd Psalm, something from the Child Craft book series that came with the World Book Encyclopedias I'd purchased a year ago. Sometimes, I told a story I'd heard or made up. This time it was the legend of old John Henry, the steel driving man who raced the machine and won. That was one of her favorites. We knelt beside her bed and said prayers and I tucked her in and turned off the light. As I walked out of the dark room and neared the door, Ella Jean sat up in her bed.

"Daddy Sloane?" She whispered. Holding on to the doorknob letting in enough light from the hallway to see her face, sweet and content, I answered. "What is it honey?"

"I love you. That's all. Night, night." She grinned.

I cleared my throat, mumbled, "I love you too," and closed the door to her room.

In the hall, I was overshadowed with emotions. The feeling of being the one that someone who could not take care of himself or herself could count on to look after them was overwhelming. It gave me unspeakable joy. I had a family. After all these years, I had a family. I admitted to myself that I had not been lonely. I was content before meeting Jean. But they say you don't know what you're missing if you never had it. This was new. It was good and it was different from anything I'd ever felt before.

My parents had been gone from this earth for so long that I'd grown accustomed to being alone. Since marrying Jean and taking care of her and Ella, I'd been so busy looking after their needs that I'd not taken time to take inventory of the impact on my life. Everything had changed. My life was full and I was a part of a new family, a family I had built with God's blessing. I was the head of a household. Husband. Father. Breadwinner. Provider. Covering.

I looked in on Jean and she was wide-awake, staring out the window with a look of longing. Something was missing. There were spaces I couldn't reach, gaping holes that I simply couldn't fill. That would be the way it was until she died. She would later drink every day and complain chronically about every aspect of the kids – and eventually me. Mean and miserable was what she became.

Everything seemed to bother her. The slightest noise was irritating. I had taken to walking Ella Jean around the block after dinner and keeping her in the kitchen coloring or drawing quietly before dinner. She played in the backyard a lot. I learned to keep my distance too. I brought dinner to her in bed but did not try to sit in our little bedroom and talk to her. I came in, removed the tray after about an hour, then washed, and dried the dishes.

In the mornings, I dressed in the bathroom as quietly as humanly possible. I kissed her goodbye on her cheek and left. She usually had little to say. If her eyes were opened, her gaze was fixed somewhere off in the distance as if she saw something I didn't see. After putting Ella to bed, I read my newspaper in the living room on the couch and then read my bible before preparing for bed. When it was time for bed, I bathed in silence again and put my pajamas on in the bathroom. Crawling into our bed, I was careful not to touch my wife. There was no holding, like before. There was no lovemaking, no intimacy and no talking. There was sleep. She lay with her back to me, cold and impenetrable, like a stone.

Now looking in on her there in the bed, being heavy with child seemed to bring about a sadness in her that carried more weight than the infant she held inside. I would come to know in eternity that she longed for her own sweet mother every day of her life. She grieved a devastating loss that I knew nothing about. I know now that Jean also suffered from severe depression. I didn't know what that was or what it looked like. I'd heard people talk about having the blues. But that in time, things would be fine. In those days, we ignored mental health problems. In our ignorance and adherence to our faith, we put a schism between faith and science that God never meant to exist. I could not reach her. I couldn't fix it. So it was the barrier between us as we waited for the baby to be born.

10

Pam was born on a Friday night after ten hours of agonizing labor. Doctor Carver met us at the Negro hospital and the lady who looked after Ella Jean, Miss Olivia, came over to sit with her. It was more hectic than I ever imagined. There was a dark energy in the waiting room as I paced back and forth that night. I was almost in a panic and I didn't know why.

Well the scripture says that when we are in the earthly realm we see through a glass darkly, as if blinded. But once enlightened, we will see as we are seen – with great clarity. I know now that both Pam and my wife, Jean, almost died that night. The umbilical cord was wrapped around the child's neck and Jean's blood pressure had spiked high. The young nurse was prompted to pray. She kept praying under her breath, mumbling something inaudible. By the time they came to the waiting room to announce that we had a healthy baby girl, Jean was exhausted. She was plumb worn out after the baby was pushed into this world.

I was taken, after what seemed like many hours, to the nursery to finally see our daughter. She was wrapped in a pink blanket, lined up in a neat row of bassinets along with other brown babies of every shade and hue. And there she was. My heart was happy! She was the most beautiful thing I'd ever laid eyes on, all wrinkled, brown, and drowsy. Things could not be any better. I prayed a prayer to God, standing there in front of the glass with the rows of bassinets and brown babies. I prayed to be the best father I could be and to protect my little girl from hurt, harm and danger.

When I arrived at my wife's room that rainy night a bitter coldness slapped me as I drew closer to the door that was cracked half opened. I heard a man's voice – low and serpent smooth. I assumed that someone must have called the pastor, but who? Maybe Miss Olivia summoned him. Pushing the door opened I realized how wrong I was. The pastor was not there, instead I found a huge blue-black man with gold teeth grinning at me. His hair was processed and slicked with pomade into a pompadour and his eyes were beet red. He stood about 6 ft. 3 inches tall with muscles bustin' out of his grey trench coat. The whole room reeked of cheap liquor as it seeped from his pores and his mouth. His wrinkled red satin shirt was opened-collared to expose a cheap gold necklace. His eyes were fixed on me as if I had interrupted something important. The small nurse rushed past me and darted down the corridor. Jean looked both terrified and tired.

"Good evening, may I help you?" I asked with puzzled pleasantness.

"Nah Captain Hero, you can't help me do shit. You done helped yo self doe, I see." His beady eyes glared and his lip turned up like an animal ready to attack.

Jean let out a little moan and tried to raise herself up in the dimly lit hospital room. The rain pounded against the window that the man stood in front of as he faced my wife. His wife. Our wife? Between her bed and him was a chair in the corner. I surveyed Jean, the chair, the man and the rain.

"Jean, who is this? Do you know this man?" My voice was low.

"Bittie Boy." Her words emerged in a whimper. She was trembling.

I moved across the room and stood between the man and the bed. So this was the long lost first husband. The sorry excuse for a man that had left my wife to raise a kid alone. This joker was back, standing in front of me.
I was surprised by the anger welling up in me. My knuckles ached.

"Perhaps we can talk outside and I can find out what my family can do for you."

I tilted my head towards the door with the expectation that he would follow. He came behind me as I had expected but pushed past me, leaving a whiff of unexplainable cold air, and walked down the hall to the exit in complete silence. Jean was crying softly in the room. I watched him shove the door with brute force and leave the hospital.

"What did he say to you? What does he want? Why is he here, Jean?"

I bombarded her with questions, angry that just when I thought I had all I ever needed, this happened. What the hell did her ex-husband want? I knew we were married legally and I had the marriage license to prove it. They had been common law husband and wife, at best, shacking up together for a couple of years. She'd been told by friends of the yellow man in the cemetery, that he'd died, been killed in a jail fight. That is what she told me while we courted and months before we married. Now here he was.

There are spirits everywhere. There are generational curses too. I would come to learn that this dark spirit would travel in many forms throughout generations of my family. Legions of demons perpetuating ill will, pain, poverty and death. I did not know that then, but I know it now.

11

Don't fret because of evildoers because they will soon be cut off and wither away like mowed grass. When I would do good, evil is always present. It is real and takes many forms. It moves timelessly executing the work of generational curses and stealing peace. Believe me when I tell you this.

Bittie Boy left the hospital that night and climbed behind the wheel of a stolen Thunderbird. *Who the hell did she think she was? Once mine, always mine* His thoughts raced as the rain beat on the windshield and he took in the happy little hospital scene burned in his memory. *She took care of me before and I'll be damned if she not gonna do it again. She don't get a meal ticket 'cause she gonna be my meal ticket.* He needed a drink.

I sat across from my wife as she sobbed and tried to tell a story, a confession of sorts about her first husband.

"He wants money." Her tiny brown hands squeezed the blanket and pulled it up around her full breasts.

"He just got out of jail and he heard about us while he was locked up. I've been dreading this day, Sloane. I knew it was just a matter of time."

"I thought you said he was dead?" I questioned, trying not to sound as if I was accusing her of lying.

"They said he was dead. He is dead. Dead to me. Dead to his baby, my baby. I got word from him that he was comin' for Ella Jean and me. I knew his being killed in a jail fight was too good to be true. Men like him don't die. They kill. "

"Jean, is this why you've been so sad lately? When did you first hear from this joker?" I needed to know.

"Three months ago he sent word that he was getting out, coming for me and the baby and things was going to be just like always. I didn't tell you because I was scared and ashamed."

She turned her face to the wall of the tiny room and just cried. Jean cried for herself. She cried for Ella Jean and for her new baby Pamela. She cried for her mother and her mother before her. But mostly she cried for women who got tangled up with men who meant them no good. Good for nothing men who didn't ever see them, only saw what they needed. The women in their lives were only a means to an end. That kind of man always found her. Until now. *But she knew it wouldn't last.*

"Don't worry about this. You are my wife and I aim to protect what is mine. That is what I aim to do. I'll take care of it."

We sat in silence for what seemed like hours until the nurse came and told me that the visiting hours were over and that I needed to make my way to the front door. I kissed my wife gently on the forehead and squeezed her hand. Holding her left hand with my ring on her finger tightly, I repeated reassurances as she lay still and defeated. I meant every word I said. I always did.

I left the hospital and the rain had slowed to a fine drizzle.

I went by the house. Miss Olivia was sitting on the couch and Ella Jean was in her bed, fast asleep. She got up and began to gather her things to leave. I asked her if she could please stay for one hour longer. She looked puzzled and asked if everything was okay with the baby and Jean. I told her both the baby and Jean were fine but there was something I had to take care of and it would only take a few minutes. She nodded and sat back down.

I went into our bedroom and reached into the top of the closet. In the very back in a corner was a metal box. I took out the contents of the box and wrapped it in a handkerchief from my top dresser drawer. It was cheap, white and had the first letter of my last name on it. I shoved it all into my overcoat inside pocket and hurriedly left the house.

I thought about where the man would be. A man like this man was thirsty. He was led by his carnal needs. I took him for a drinking man and unless he had friends or a woman in town, he was at Pete's Place, the bar that black folks claimed as their neighborhood watering hole. It was small and musty and they watered down the drinks, but it was open late night and all day. There was a pool table in the back and weekly card games on Friday night. I felt that would be a good place to look first. I was right. Something had led me to the right spot.

I opened the door and there in the corner of the "L" shaped bar was my man. The guy who thought he was going to intimidate and bully my wife. I would come to know his story beyond the grave, but for now, he was someone that sparked a rage in me that was difficult to contain. I adjusted my eyes to the smoke filled room and walked over to the man. He had seen me come in and he was staring as I approached.

It was almost as if he'd been expecting me.

"Well if it isn't Captain Hero." He snarled as I came near.

"Stay away from my wife. Do you understand?" The directive was basic. I meant what I said.

Your wife? What is mine is always mine. Besides, who's going to see that I do?" Bittie Boy chuckled in defiance.

"Stay away from my wife. Do you understand?" The directive was the same. It was plain.

"I heard about you and how you was gonna make a kept woman out of my workhorse. Man you better get out of here before you get hurt."

He threw his cigarette on the bar floor and put it out with his rocked over dress shoes.

I pulled out the handkerchief from my coat pocket and placed it next to his empty whiskey glass.

"You look like a man who needs money, who loves money and will do most anything for it. This is $500. It's all I got. It's all you ever gone get from me. It comes with some strings attached."

He reached for the money with a grin. I slammed my hand down on it before he could pick it up. Patting my coat, I was as frank as I could be with this man.

"You say you heard about me. Well I also heard about you. When your yellow friend tried to rape Jean and started coming around her house, I did some asking around about you. I put a tail on you and in my pocket is an envelope. In that envelope are dates, times and witnesses. You already know the crimes. You know what you did time for but you also know what you think you got away with."

"You're lying. Bert wouldn't cross me. You're bluffing. I call bullshit. You ain't got nothin' on me. "

His red eyes burned into my face. He was mad. But he was also scared. Most bullies are cowards and he was no different.

"The gas station robbery in Tupelo, the burglary of Dr. Henry Wright's home in Birmingham, the man you and Bert robbed in Selma and Lily, do you remember Lily? Do you remember what you and Bert did to her? Bert does. I have dates. I have witnesses. Names. Am I bluffing?"

I pushed the money towards him.

"The evidence is in someone else's hands. The instructions are simple. If anything happens to me, to Jean or Ella Jean, they are handed to the police and you get to return to prison. You are a marked man."

He put the money in his pocket and continue to stare in defiance. Perhaps he didn't understand. The bar was near empty and the bartender was busy trying to pretend not to listen. The music was low. It was B.B. King number. I needed him to understand. Leaning closer into this broken bully of a man, I whispered.

"I love that woman and that little girl. I aim to protect them. I am a God fearing man. But I will kill you without so much as a thought if you ever come near or have any contact with my family."

I walked to the door of the bar; not wanting to hear what he had to say. I half expected him to come after me. He didn't. Spiritual warfare is real. I was reminded of the passage, "Greater is he that is in me, than he that is in the world." The rain had let up and I drove home to relieve Miss Olivia of her duties and to thank her for staying.

We never heard from Bittie Boy again. I heard he died in a botched robbery at a filling station in Mobile several years later. I wasn't certain that was true, but I know now he died an awful death. I see him in the sunken place even now.

12

Life for our little family moved into a sweet routine. Jean appeared to be happy for a while. She cared for the baby and even came back to the table and started taking her meals with Ella and me. She watched the baby, I took Ella Jean to the babysitter's the same as before. I didn't want her to get overwhelmed. I came home, made dinner, and did the dishes. She was in the bedroom less and more tender with Ella Jean.

Ella Jean marveled at her mother with the baby. She saw a side of Jean that she didn't recognize. It made the little girl happy. She was proud to be a big sister and overwhelmed with the joy and contentment of a loving family. It was new to her but she loved everything about it and watched each interaction with amazement. When she saw me kiss her mother and joke with her and Jean laugh from somewhere deep in her gut at something I said, Ella was wide eyed with wonder. When she heard Jean singing and rocking Pam for the first time, she just stood at her mother's knee grinning. She was learning a new language. It was love.

Jean was grateful that the threat of the man that made her life miserable was over. I did not know the details of it because she never talked about it. I didn't ask about him either. It was her past and I was a big enough man not to force her to relive it. I simple told her when I went to the hospital the next morning, after paying Bittie Boy, that she would never hear from him again. At first, she didn't believe me. I promised her and that was a promise I was able to keep. She became more relaxed every day that he didn't show up at our door. The yellow man Bert was gone too. She finally felt safe.

I would learn beyond this life that the man had put her through unspeakable horrors. He'd refused to work and forced her to clean houses as a domestic and occasionally sleep with men for money. He'd taken every dime she made and spent it on booze, gambling and his other women. Worst of all, Bittie Boy had been angry that Jean had "let herself" get pregnant. He didn't want to be a father. He had five kids peppered through Alabama and Mississippi and took care of none of them. He didn't want to lose his workhorse. I'd come to know that he bragged to his friend about her and called her just that – his "old work horse."

So we went along like that. Work during the week, church on Sundays and a few friends from church who would come over some Friday nights and sit, talk, and play cards. They'd bring their kids and the kids played outside in the front or the back yard for hours. They'd play freeze tag, mother may I, and as they grew up, dodge ball and kick ball. It was a good life for a while.

About the time Pam started school, when she was around five or six years old, things began to change. Ella was nine or ten and the changes in Jean seemed to come out of the blue. Jean's moods changed frequently. She stopped going to church. She stayed in bed more often and withdrew from the family. Worst of all, Jean started drinking again. I don't know if the drinking came first and led to the other behaviors or if the withdrawal made her want to drink. She would fly off the handle and get angry with the girls for the least little thing. At times, nothing pleased her. Other times she seemed ecstatic and really bold as if she was unstoppable.

It was frightening for the girls. I kept them away from her as best I could. Doing homework together at the table or in their rooms. Ella instinctively protected her little sister Pam. I quit going to the NAACP field meetings or the monthly trustee board meetings at church. If I did go, I took the girls with me or dropped them off at their old babysitter, Miss Olivia's house. They became close in their shared misery. I did what I could but I couldn't fix it.

Friends and acquaintances were no longer welcome to the house. A part of it was because I couldn't predict what mood she'd be in and a part of it was because I wanted to protect both she and the girls from the small town gossip I knew would come. It was that way until Jean died.

She got progressively worse. The doctors said there was nothing wrong with her. It was all in her head. She needed rest. Wean her off alcohol or send her to the asylum was what the last doctor said. I couldn't do that. The place they took colored women in those days was not fit for a dog. They were poorly treated, experimented on and often raped and neglected. I couldn't send her there. So I shielded her from curious eyes and the girls from her and took care of all of them as best I could.

The Present

"No one who has left home or brothers or sisters or mother or father or children or fields for me and the gospel [30] will fail to receive a hundred times as much in this present age"

Matthew 10:29-3

13

My granddaughter, Rene' was the one I had a keen eye on. Evil didn't die; it only reinvented itself over and over again, taking on many forms. Always with the same end goal - to kill, rob and destroy.

Rene' was nervous about meeting Jackson, her ex-husband's boss. She had information that he needed to know. The idea of the meeting had chased her down until she felt she had no choice. She stopped running from it. At first, she thought she'd talk to her father. But her father had been hurt enough by this mess and had the physical scars to prove it. She would follow military protocol and speak with her ex-husbands direct supervisor. Jackson was his last commanding officer.

Raegan had agreed to pick up Parker from his preschool and let him hang out at her house until she got back. She'd told her husband that she had a client to see in Norfolk. He was expecting her after seven o'clock. Lately, it seemed all Rene' did was lie. It pained her but she had to do what she had to do. She consoled herself by comparing her lies to Esther's in the bible. She did what she had to do. *Wise as a serpent, harmless as a dove* and all that stuff. She laughed into the silence of her empty SUV.

She arrived on time for their meeting and showed her driver's license to clear the gate. Norfolk Naval Base was huge, but it was painfully familiar. Wearing a black skirt and

matching shell and cardigan with black heeled boots; she could easily have been dressed for a funeral. Her only jewelry was a single strand of pearls and pearl stud earrings. Her hair was loose and hung on her shoulders, it was held off her face with a black velvet headband. She walked with a clipped pace to the outer office of Admiral Jackson McDonald.

Rene' cleared security and sat waiting for Jackson to come out and get her. His secretary was a civilian government worker but everyone else she saw buzzing about was in uniform.

"Mrs. Green, Admiral McDonald will see you now."

The short older woman with red hair and matching lips led her to the door and opened it. The room was large and Jackson waited for her to close the door before coming around his desk and enveloping Rene' in his arms. The hug felt warm and familiar. He was like an uncle, one of her father's closest friends.

"Sweetheart, how are you? You get more beautiful each time I see you. What brings this old man such good fortune today?"

"I'm good. You look amazing, all decked out with your fourth star! Can I hug a fourth star like this? Is this a breach of protocol?" She teased him.

They both sat down, Jackson at his desk and Rene' in one of two large blue Queen Anne winged back chairs in front of his desk. He stared intently waiting to find out what was going on. Rene' cleared her throat.

"First you have to promise that this conversation is between you and me. You can't tell my father. Ever. He will worry and get in the middle of it. He is retired and finally relaxed. You cannot tell him. You cannot tell Anne, even though she is your wife and I love her like an aunt. Anne can't know because she will tell Pam. Pam cannot know because she will worry and tell my sisters. My sisters, Anne and Pam will freak out and cause more crazy than I can take right now. Do you promise?"

Rene' waited for Jackson to respond.

"Yes. What is it?"

"What would be the charges levied against my husband, were he alive?"

"Is that what this is about? Jared? Rene', he's dead. NCIS confirmed his death with dental records after the crash. He was declared legally dead three years ago."

Jackson was definitive in his tone. Rene' repeated her question as if she hadn't heard anything he said.

"What would be the charges levied against him be if he was alive?"

She'll pulled an envelope from her black Tori Burch tote that sat on the floor next to her chair.

"This is all theoretical. Well, initially he would have been AWOL and if he'd turned himself in, there would have been a court marshal and considering your father, there would have been leniency. "

Rene' nodded and leaned in.

"And now? Now that it's been three years?"

"He is in violation of article 85 of the Uniform Code of Military Justice. That has to do with desertion. He is also in violation of article 87 because he left during a military assignment. Therefore, he's missing in movement, which is a further and serious violation of the UCMJ. Finally, if it can be proven that he was selling information to the Russians, he's looking at an article 106A infraction. That deals with espionage violations. Jared would be looking at life in prison."

Rene' placed the envelope on the desk. Jackson opened it. His face turned as white as sheet.

"I know I'm not crazy, even though Tony thinks I am. I am often followed and I know he's watching me. You are looking at pages of dates and times and patterns. You are looking at proof. I don't know whose dental records those were or who identified them as Jared's. But I know he's not dead. Jared Foster Reed is very much alive."

14

Trouble was brewing. Sometimes you think you have moved on and you haven't. Things were not as healed as they seemed. Some wounds are just deep. But I also know how it will end.

Rene' answered the doorbell. The guys were there on time. She had things to do and she hoped they'd work fast. Jackson advised her to change the alarm system and she convinced Tony that they needed to do so. She knew he thought she was losing her mind but she'd have to pay that price for now.

"Morning ma'am. We're looking for the Dr. Anthony Green residence. We got an installation today. Are you Mrs. Green?"

"Yes, come on in. I've been expecting you."

Rene' ushered three nondescript guys into the house and showed them to the electric power sources they asked about. She retreated to the kitchen where she had been working on a profit and loss statement for a client to finish her work before she had to pick up her son from daycare.

Parker went Mondays, Wednesdays and some Fridays from nine o'clock until noon just for socialization. It was a good break for both of them and gave her more time for her financial consulting clients.

The largest of the three men was the lead dog. He prompted the other two to cover their feet with the cloth shoe covers to protect the floor and then he seemed to give a string of nonverbal signals as instructions. They laid out toolboxes, worked from the garage to the kitchen, and went to each room in the house. They worked quickly and quietly.

"Ma'am, we're done. The keypad works just like the old one that we replaced. You just have to program the new codes into the system. Could you sign this invoice? You have thirty days to remit payment and we'll be outcher hair."

Rene' signed the invoice, took her copy and closed the door behind the guys. She watched them pile into the van before going to the kitchen to finish her work. In exactly two hours, she needed to leave to go pick up her son.

The three men did not drive the truck to the next job and they didn't take it back to the company garage either. They drove for 30 minutes, all three sitting in the front seat of the white company cargo van. They turned into a small semicircle of houses off a country road and turned the engine off.

They approached the unlocked door and went inside the dirty room.

"Is the job done?" A tall man asked, hand held out.

"Yep. We gone give you your shirts, get in our car and be on our way. It was a pleasure doing business with you boys again." The lead dog spoke.

He counted out ten crisp hundred-dollar bills into the man's open palm and they began removing the company clothes they had borrowed and putting on their own. They left the house and drove away in a grey sedan.

The guys in the house sat around with the TV blaring some news show until the man with the money gave each of them their cut and said it was time to go to work installing alarm systems.

"This is sweet. How often y'all do this?" The newest man on the team spoke up.

"Every now and then. Small side hustle, it didn't happen – okay?" The guy nodded.

Outside the grey car drove along with the three men who had been inside of Rene's house.

"So why did Joe want the spy-ware in in the black doctor's house? I heard he's watching the house too." The guy in the back spoke up.

"Something about his dead brother's wife. "

15

Taking care of Jean reminds me of the things that other men couldn't get right. I have watched my people. Even when I wasn't trying to I saw them. I felt them. I advocated beyond their realm for them. I saw Jared watching my granddaughter and great grandson. I witnessed the rebuilding of Rene's life and I knew the threat. I saw it all.

In the predawn darkness, Jared sat staring at the computer screen wanting to touch every inch of the little boy's face smiling directly at him. This was his son. Rene' had named him Parker. He had countless photos of him. She had given him Tony's last name and he had no idea that his real father even existed. That hurt the most.

Rene' had recently gotten Jackson McDonald on his ass. She just wouldn't stop. There was a leak somewhere. He would find it and plug it. Jared pounded his fist on the bamboo desk and immediately regretted it. He didn't want to wake Kata. The last thing he needed was her asking questions. Lately she seemed more suspicious and a little uneasy about everything.

He waited motionless at the desk listening for any movement coming from behind the closed bedroom door. The small flat was comfortable. Kata was comfortable, but she wasn't Rene'. He heard nothing, she didn't move, or so he thought.

"Michael, what are you doing up baby?"

Kata appeared from nowhere and stood silently in the doorframe. Jared added hating when she called him baby to the growing list of things that had begun to agitate him about his newest temporary girlfriend. Switching the image of the boy on the screen with the tap of a key, he looked away from the colorful display of cards against the green background.

"Playing solitaire. I couldn't sleep. Why are you up? Did I wake you?'

Kata came toward him in the darkened room, illuminated only by the light of the screen. She stood with bare feet and a white cotton nightgown with three open buttons revealing much of her tiny breast. Before he could speak, again she was behind him, rubbing his shoulders. This was the price he paid for living a lie. He lost everything. Kata's presence was a constant reminder. Even when they made love, he thought only of Rene'.

Jared clicked the power off and shut the laptop cover down gently. He stood, forcing the woman to let go of his shoulder, abruptly halting the annoying massage.

"Let's go back to bed; it's three o'clock in the morning. Sorry I woke you up." He led as she followed in silence. They climbed into their shared bed and Kata snuggled close to him, her arm across his chest. She talked about their future together. He listened and lied enough to keep living rent free and getting free sex. He was ready to go. Jared lay flat on his back with his eyes closed waiting for the sun to come up. Waiting to get away from the woman next to him.

No one was taking his son, not Tony and Rene', not even

the powerful Hamilton family. They thought he was dead and that they would live happily ever after. He thought that too. He thought he'd live happily ever after. But the problem with happily ever after is that everybody defines it differently. Jared was stubborn and determined. There was no happily ever after without *his* son and *his* wife.

He knew he had messed up. To hell with her father. All this tight knit family bullshit was something they could miss him with. He didn't have it, hadn't known it and wasn't going to waste any more time trying to fit into it. Jared had grown tired of being the poor white boy among these uppity black folks. He thought assimilating into their world would have been easier. He underestimated everything. In the final analysis, it was less about race and more about experiences, exposure and culture. Screw it all. He wanted his wife, his child and his name back. The rest of them could kiss his poor white, murdering ass. He was going to win in the end.

Up until now, Admirals McDonald and Hamilton, along with the Naval Criminal Investigative Services (NCIS) thought he was dead. The deals were done and he was alive. Kata was a placeholder and nothing more. The plan had never changed, even though there had been a few minor issues. Originally, he thought he'd send for Rene' and the baby when he got settled. He hadn't planned on Dr. Tony Green, the childhood friend, the fellow fucking "Jack and Jiller" (whatever that shit meant) swooping in and marrying his wife. He hadn't planned to return to the states, but he hadn't planned to be declared legally dead. He thought she'd wait for a while, at least. Rene' began seeing Tony with a quickness and moved on with her life. Now he had to regroup and show up and if necessary, show out.

They were all planning to spend Christmas together as a family at Pam and Randolph's home in the small, rural Pungo area of Virginia Beach. They would have their hallmark, holiday, hearth and home and all that shit. It worked for him, because his plan was to spend Christmas with his family too. He would finally see his boy, his son and reunite with his beautiful wife. He'd be there too. Bet money.

16

Rene' poured the organic oats into the boiling pot of water and cinnamon and began to stir. She felt strange and wasn't sure why. She had the eerie feeling that she was being watched. Lately there had been an uneasiness that she couldn't explain. She'd told no one, not even her husband, Tony. Dipping oatmeal into a small black and white Mackenzie Childs toddler bowl, she glanced out the kitchen window and saw only trees. The neighborhood kids were all in school by now. It was nine o'clock. She placed the bowl and the matching spoon on the table with a white napkin folded into a triangle and went to the kitchen staircase or as Parker called it, "the back stairs".

"Parker, come eat your breakfast buddy".

On cue, Parker emerged grinning at the top of the short staircase, wearing Osh Gosh overalls and red socks with trains on them. His chubby baby fingers clutching his red high top sneakers with one hand and dragging a red and blue sweater on the floor with the other hand. He never walked. He always ran and was the happiest little three year old she had ever seen.

Parker Randolph Green bore the middle name of his grandfather and the last of her husband, Dr. Tony Green – the man he called "daddy". Tony was the only father he had every known and the man in the hospital with her at his birth.

After she was shot by an unknown assailant (per the police report) at her father's change of command ceremony, Tony had never left her side. He had been there for her. Tony explained to her the horrible plan her manipulative dead cousin Michelle had put in place, after she showed him all of the illicit and graphic texts messages allegedly sent by him to her. He could trace the date to the times he'd spent with her and naively left his phone unattended and unlocked. Michelle had lied out of sheer jealousy and evilness.

But Parker was alive and beautiful. He was the only good thing to come from her first marriage. Tony and Rene' were married in a private ceremony with only their families in attendance, shortly after the baby was born. Rene' made the decision to allow Tony to adopt Parker when he was 3 months old. His name changed legally before he ever had the chance to learn anything different. Dr. Tony Green was the only father he knew. Rene' felt this was her second chance and she was determined to love and live. She was determined to be happy.

Parker was born in the midst of tragedy. His biological father, masterminded the plan and had no idea, it would harm his wife and unborn child more than his planned target. It reminded Rene' of something her aunt Ella Jean always said. "When you dig a hole for someone, you might as well dig two." The implication was real to her the first time she heard this at about nine years old. She processed it as don't set crazy traps for other people because you will inevitably be caught in them too. This had indeed happened. It was such a mess. But God. She tried not to think about any of it. He must never know any of it. It made her feel sick thinking about it.

Parker was the spitting image of Jared. There was no escaping that. His white father's genetic composition was all over Rene's son. His eyes were hazel but framed exactly like his biological father's eyes, his hairline, his facial features, and his walk all spoke to his true identity. But nothing was more like his father, than his smile. He had the most beautiful smile and he laughed with his entire face.

Rene' was brown with shoulder length curly hair and Tony was deep chocolate. She was aware that most people thought Parker to be their adopted son. She never confirmed or denied it. She left it all alone. Her job was to love and raise her son. This was her happily ever after and she had almost missed it.

She put both arms out and caught her baby as he raced down the stairs. Catching the sweater and shoes and the curly headed boy, Rene' planted kisses on his sand colored cheeks. He was so soft, so warm, and so good. Parker was proof positive that there was a God. Just thinking about him made her happy. He was a gift.

"Whose boy is this? She gobbled up his little boy face as she placed him in his chair.

"I'm Parker, your boy!" Parker giggled and wiggled out of her embrace.

The only good thing Jared had given her was Parker. He was the sweetest part of each day and the joy of her new life.

"Eat your oatmeal Parker so we can go into the city and meet Daddy."

Parker grabbed the spoon and began eating the oatmeal with cinnamon, raisins and almond milk. It was his favorite breakfast. Rene' placed the opened Annie's organic apple juice box down in front of him when the bowl was almost empty. His chubby fingers grabbed it and began drinking the juice from the tiny straw. She cleared the empty bowl and freed Parker from his high chair. Rene' washed and dried his breakfast dishes while Parker sat digging through a basket of wooden trains and trucks near the staircase. Moving quietly from the six-burner stove to grab the pot, rinse it and place it in the dishwasher, Rene' felt happy. She had a new life and it was a good life.

Their home in McLean, Virginia sat on a wooded two-acre lot, with most of the land in the back of the house. Rene' stared blankly out of the window in front of her farmhouse kitchen sink. It was the beginning of fall and the trees were starting to put on their spectacular color show. Orange, reds, yellows and browns created an amazing sight. Directly within view was the fire pit with the Adirondack chairs circling it and not far from it was Parker's wooden swing set and slide. A few feet away was the fort with the sandbox beneath it. It was covered with a blue plastic lid so the neighbor's cats wouldn't use it as a litter box. Beyond that was a tennis court and to the left of the court, a small two bedroom guesthouse and the covered pool. There was nothing moving. Silence. Then she saw him. A shadowy figure moved quickly from behind the guesthouse.

Rene' scooped Parker up from his knees scooting a wooden car along the travertine floor and barreled for the backdoor. She stood on the deck and yelled,

"Who's there? This is private property!"

Silence. Stillness. Parker laughed, thinking her swift movements signaled a game. He was staring in her face as she stood surveying the property.

Rene' walked back across the deck to the back door. As she placed her hand on the knob, she heard rustling in the trees. Her head snapped back in the direction of the noise. She saw no one. She went back into the kitchen, bolted the door, and locked the dead bolt. Checking the alarm in the hallway to make sure it was on; she went to the front of the house where she could check the road for cars, her baby in her arms, oblivious to any danger. She recognized the cars in each driveway.

The front double doors were decorative beveled glass. There were no cars on the street. Everything seemed normal. The front door was locked. Rene' went back to the kitchen, put the squirming toddler down on the floor, and reached for her cell phone on the kitchen counter. Standing in front of the window at the kitchen sink, she punched rapidly until the phone rang.

"Hey babe, I'm on the move making rounds and will be there in 30 minutes."
"Are you on your way?" Tony's voice was warm and soothing.

"No, I'm still at home and I know I'll be late, about to leave in a minute but, I think someone was out back watching the house, Tony." Rene' didn't want to alarm him.

"Call the police." The warmth from his voice was suddenly replaced with anger.

"No, I'm coming into the city. We had planned to take Parker to the Smithsonian train exhibit and today is the last day. Let's do it. My parents will be here late tonight and I don't want my mom to get all alarmed. You know she worries about *everything*. The alarm is on. See you in thirty minutes."

Rene' spoke with a casual resolve, waited for Tony's okay and ended the call.

17

Everything done in the dark eventually comes to the light. I know that and I learned it early and easy. Some people are not so fortunate. All of their lessons are hard ones.

Kata lay beside Michael and wondered why he thought she was so dumb. Did she look dumb? Was it just her or was it all women? His words were sweet but his heart was insincere and he needed her for shelter and comfort only. Kata made it easier for him to blend into the landscape and go undetected. Amused, she thought of herself as his camouflage uniform.

She wondered though why he thought he could use her. Why he thought their lopsided arrangement fulfilled all her needs. The truth was he didn't care. Men like him thought people were disposable. Blinded by his own desires, he didn't see her and she knew it. Michael looked right through her, past her. He thought he knew her so well, just a simple girl from the countryside. He thought he knew everything. But she knew more about him than he knew about her and she

had played the games he was trying to play for longer and better. Growing impatient, she tried to calm herself and to remain cool and steady. It was her trademark. She had to stick with the plan.

"Michael, what are you thinking love? Or as you Americans say, a penny for your thoughts."

She pretended to smile knowing that the darkness would not reveal her face nor her truth. She waited for him to lie.

"Thinking about us, babe. I was thinking about the life we're going to have when we get back to the states."

"Tell me more honey; I always like to hear your dreams. I know it's going to be a wonderful life. Will I find work or just make babies with you?" She cooed.

Kata could feel his body bristle and stiffen, revealing his true repulsion at having children together. It brought her some small joy to make him uncomfortable.

"You can do whatever your heart desires. As long as we're together, that's all that matters. I promise we'll be happy. I have more money than we will ever need. Get some sleep, its three o'clock in the morning."

Jared lied without blinking an eye. It was easy. It was natural.

Kata kissed his cheek and moved in closer to his body. She rubbed his bare chest and closed her eyes praying for sleep to come. She told herself, this would be the last one, the last time. She was getting too old and she was ready to settle down. Her parents wanted her to come and live with them and she was warming up to the idea of being closer to her sisters and brothers and going back to the place she'd lived as a younger woman. A place where people loved and lived in simplicity, a place where she was known as Anna.

What started out as an effort to make a little money many

years ago had grown into something bigger with each passing year. Now here she was. Entangled with this man, living this lie that she knew all too well. Eugene, Michael, Jared Foster Reed, they are all the same.

18

Ella Jean was finally happy. Hers had been a life with more than its share of pain. I watched Ella Jean sit in her old kitchen that was bursting with blossoms and shades of blue not found in nature. The best word for it was "busy". The wallpaper was large baby blue and royal blue floral prints. She was surrounded by neatly stacked boxes of dishes, glasses and pots and pans. Her chin rested on her cupped hand propped up by her elbow on the cool blue vinyl placemat.

This had been my home. The home I brought Ella Jean and my wife Jean to after we were married. Even in its brokenness, the union was an answer to many unspoken prayers. I was lonelier than I understood or knew. I needed a wife and more importantly those two little girls to care for. They were my destiny. Ella Jean had taken over the home after my death. She was the last man standing, so to speak and the keeper of the legacy.

Ella Jean was all grown up and she had gotten through the roughest parts of her life. She would still have some trials, but there was so much sweetness in her future. She had endured so much and sown many good seeds through it all. This was her season of reaping and I was so proud of her. If anybody deserved happiness, she did.

Ella looked at her arm and marveled at its size. She'd lost nearly fifty pounds since her marriage to Moses. They walked and talked in the morning and that was more activity than she'd had in years. Then there was the sex. Good Lord, the sex. Ella Jean loved the lovin'. Every part of it was special and new to her. The kissing and waking up enveloped in Moses' arms was more than she'd ever expected. She'd never in her life been touched like that or the center of anybody's intentions in a loving way. She let out a sigh of pleasure just thinking about the goodness in her new life. Sheba had a forever home with her and Moses, following them from room to room. The little dog was a sweet reminder of the goodness in Michelle.

Staring out the window at the coolness of autumn, she felt relieved to be finally moving into her new home. Moses said it was time to put the "new wine in new wine skins." It was a joke, a "bible" joke. He had lots of them, based on his favorite passages. She loved how they laughed at stuff like that and even though she had worked for him for many years, she'd never known this side of him. He had been friendly, but mostly serious. Now that they were married, everything was different – everything was better.

Ella whispered, "new" as if hearing the words would make it all seem real. The movers were scheduled to arrive at 10:00 giving her exactly one hour to gather the last of the bed linens from the dryer and pack them up. They'd lived the last two years in her house because she'd wanted to take her time to find a forever home. They had settled on having a brand new home built on three acres of land. Ella would finally have the large vegetable and flower garden she had always wanted. Her husband, Reverend Moses Franklin would be waiting at the new house to blend her household goods with his as the final act of living this new life. She'd been the church secretary for years and helped him raise his son, Frankie Bea. Now she was his wife and she could not quite believe it.

Ella Jean Franklin thought about how her life had changed since Michelle's death. Ella Jean's only daughter had died in the hospital of cardiac arrest after a tragic car accident. Her death was hard enough to take, but was confounded by the fact that her diary revealed that she'd been having an affair with her cousin Rene's husband, Jared. Ella felt ashamed of her child and just embarrassed that she would bring so much pain to her niece, her younger sister, Pam's daughter.

In the beginning, the grief was unbearable. It was ugly. Soaked and stained pillows marked her sleepless nights and the days found her completing daily tasks like a robot whose batteries were low. She was in her small home, the one she'd spent her first four years in, the one where she had suffered unspeakable abuse. Only her body was there. In the days that followed Michelle's death, the core of who she was, her spirit, mind and soul were always with her daughter. She saw Michelle's beautiful face and thick curly hair everywhere. A healthy dose of guilt seemed to come along with motherhood. Ella Jean felt it every second of every day. She worried that she had failed as a mother, that somehow Michelle's death was her fault.

If she had been more honest with Michelle about her father maybe, she wouldn't have craved the love of a man so much that she was willing to be someone's mistress. Ella thought about being raped and abused by her once adored college professor, Dr. Michael Montgomery. She had wanted to tell Michelle about her father, her broken beginning, so many times. How do you tell a child something like that? After escaping the good doctor's back room abortion planned for her child and surviving his final and most brutal beating, Ella decided to raise her baby by herself in the home she had been rescued from by Daddy Sloane.

She moved into her mother's original small home that

Daddy Sloane had purchased outright when he moved them out of it into his small brick house. It had become rental property and extra income for the family of four. Daddy Sloane was smart with money that way. When she came home pregnant and Pam was preparing to move away to go to college, Daddy Sloane suggested she move into the house. Ella knew now that it was his effort to get the baby away from Jean and give Ella a chance to bond with her baby, to parent Michelle without interference.

She felt now that it had been a mistake, not keeping her baby, but coming back to Pascagoula, Mississippi. Maybe it was too small for her ambitious daughter. They were alone in the house with the sad past. Ella Jean often wondered if she'd moved away to Birmingham or Atlanta if things would have been different. She'd wanted a father figure for her baby and Daddy Sloane was all she had. Living in the same town with him gave her support and family. He had been her hero and the buffer created between her and her drunken mother.

The home was for sale now. Frankie Bea, her stepson didn't want it. He had a sustainable farm in the county and Ella had decided she had no further use for the house. They'd had a few people come by to look at it and Rev felt confident, it would be sold within the next few months. She'd planned to give the money from the sale to the church because she didn't need it. With the surprise inheritance from Michelle's father, she had more money than she would ever need. Things had turned out in a way she could never have predicted. Life sure was funny.

The phone rang and interrupted the flow of her thoughts. It was what it was. She'd done the best she could by Michelle. Her death was an accident. Her heart gave out after the trauma of the accident. But Michelle's death also had to do with greed, lust, adultery and her own demons.

Confirming this mentally as she answered the phone was good for Ella Jean, even if she wasn't totally convinced it wasn't all her fault. Picking up the baby blue princess wall phone, she immediately began to smile.

"Hey, hey Sadie the married lady", Pam chided.

"Hey baby sister, how you doing? What's going on?" Ella was happy to hear her sister's voice on the other end of the phone.

"Girl, I'm waiting for Randolph. He went to gas up the car. We are driving up to D. C. for Gracie's christening and to spend a couple of days with the kids. I need to see my Parker and baby Gracie as often as I can. They grow so fast and I don't want to miss a thing! I have talked to everybody except for Tony and Rene'. I can't reach either of them on the phone. I sent a text giving them our estimated time of arrival because we're using their house as the command central this time. We'll sleep there and gather with the others. But I got nothing back and Rene's phone goes straight to voicemail. I don't want to get the girls involved. I think Rae is on business travel anyway. So, I'm going to just…." Pam went on an exasperated rant.

"Pam, breathe. You're getting worked up. You know they get busy. Don't worry. Rene' will get back to you." Ella reassured her younger sister, something she had been doing most of her life.

"That could be it, but I don't know why they aren't picking up the phone."

"God is in it Pam, he sits high and looks low and has not given you a spirit of fear. Everything is fine."

Ella Jean spoke comfort in soft tones. It was late September and everybody was looking forward to spending Christmas with Pam and Randolph in Virginia Beach. Ella Jean wanted this to be a safe time and a good time for the whole family. So much had changed in the past few years. She was looking forward to a get away with her new husband after setting up their brand new house. They said their goodbyes and she waited for the moving van to help her close the final door in her old life.

19

Reagan had suffered much loss. …...miscarriages and finally Grace was born. She and her husband Sean were happy and very much in love. They didn't attend church regularly but prayed, read the scriptures and believed. She was the most intuitive of them all. She trusted her gut, which some would come to term, the Holy Spirit.

Grace was napping and Reagan had plans to get her up soon, so they could pick up Parker from preschool. Grace would be thrilled to know that she had an afternoon play date with Parker. Rene' sounded so stressed when she'd asked her. She had to work tonight but Rene' said she'd be back by 6:00. Sean would be there and would give the babies dinner if her sister wasn't back in time.

She taught four classes each week and only one evening class. The art history lecture would be over at 10:00 and she'd be home by 11:00 if no students lingered. She'd have to keep the pace up on the "goodbye see you next week" at the end of class, especially for the boys. Two or three every year thought they were grown enough as juniors in undergrad to "holler" at the professor. She smirked and mumbled, "Not today, Satan."

Reagan heard Grace stirring on the baby monitor on the granite kitchen counter. Barefoot in ripped jeans and an orange cotton camisole she unlatched the baby gate and climbed the stairs toward Grace's room. The bamboo toddler bed stood in the center of the lemon yellow room with murals of animals on three of the four walls and "God's Grace" spelled out in huge mint green letters on the fourth wall.

The round sepia face sitting up in the bed was the most delicious mixture of Sean and Reagan. Grace broke into a sweet grin and reached out for her mother. Reagan almost felt dizzy and overwhelmed with the blessing of motherhood. Intoxicated was the word she used. She and Sean teased that they were "Grace drunk". She was everything. They had waited so long and there had been too many miscarriages and too much guilt about them.

"Hey Grace, face! What's up?"

Reagan kissed her daughter and sent her down the hall to use the potty.

"I be back in a minute, kay?

Grace bolted down the hall with a crown of thick black kinky hair wild about her head wearing purple cotton panties and a matching t-shirt.

At two and a half, Grace knew her colors, letters and numbers to 10. Purple was her current favorite color. The letter "S" was her favorite letter because it was like a snake. The number "2" was her favorite number and the quantity she wanted to have of everything. She needed two. Grace wanted to point out the s's she saw everywhere. Purple was the color she wanted her ribbon, barrettes and clothes to be.

"Let's wash your hands and get dressed, Boo bear. I have a surprise for you." Reagan called after her daughter.

Grace was already on the stool at the sink washing her hands, using a week's worth of liquid soap, dispensed from a plastic giraffe dispenser. When she was all cleaned up, Reagan scooped her baby into her arms and took her back to her room to get dressed.

"Guess where we're going?"

Reagan asked as she pulled a purple dress with an organza tutu at the bottom over her daughter's head.

"The library?"

Reagan shook her head no.

"Art class?"

Again, the mother signaled no.

"Chuckie Cheese?"

Reagan laughed.

"We are going to pick up Parker from school and he's coming to our house to play for the whole day!"

Grace squealed and jumped up to find her rain boots. There was not a cloud in sight but they were her current favorite footwear.

"Yeah! Parker's coming to see me! I'm gonna give him two kisses and teach him how to make the letter S and write his name and dance ballet. And sing. And make a purple sun."

20

My only biological daughter was happy. She hadn't changed much since she was a little girl. She always wanted to help, wanted to serve and save the world. I was pleased with her husband, a fine fellow. I'd met some of his people in eternity and he came from good stock. My Pam still had a thorn in her side and some dark days ahead, but she had grown into a woman of great faith and beauty.

Randolph came in through the garage door and called to her.

"You ready Pam? We need to get on the road."

Pam wasn't exactly ready but she was excited because she loved road trips with her husband. He said she was the perfect first mate and she was. Easily distracted by her own thoughts, Pam found driving laborious. But she was the perfect DJ with some classical music, old Motown, some jazz standards like Nancy Wilson and Ella Fitzgerald and his all-time favorites, Al Green and Mahalia Jackson. Plus she was always equipped with the best road trip snacks. In her basket on the center of the back seat were cashews, trail mix, carrots and all kinds of dried and fresh fruit. Watching the world pass, reading billboards and listening to music was relaxing and suited her just fine. She stuffed the last few items in her already packed suitcase, sat on it to zip it, and left it on the bed.

She padded down the wooden stairs to greet her husband of over 36 years. Randolph was smiling at the foot of the staircase taking it all in. His wife with a pink sweater tied neatly over her crisp white blouse moved swiftly towards him. Her blouse was tucked neatly into khaki pants that hugged her hips. The pants didn't have pockets and they zipped on the side. He never understood the side zipper, seemed like an awful trick played on women by sadistic fashion designers. He knew his 59-year-old bladder wouldn't make it if he had to fiddle and fumble with a side zipper. He drank in her energy. Her beautiful face, soft and brown did not look like that of a 58-year-old woman. Her brown bob flipping about her face as she came towards him broadened his smile into a grin. She was beautiful and full of life; he still felt like the luckiest man in the world when he saw her.

"What? Okay Randolph, stop grinning and get my bags sir. The darn thing was too heavy to lift. I've got the christening outfit and packed presents for both of my babies."

Pam pecked him on the cheek landing on the bottom step as he stood firmly on the floor in front of the staircase. He wrapped both arms around her, patted her butt and moved her to the side to climb the stairs and get the bags.

"I hope you didn't pack a steamer trunk, Pam. We are only staying two days." He called from the top of the steps.

"Just one small bag and a garment bag. That's all." She moved past the living room with overstuffed beige silk sofas and mahogany table, then the dining room with the large Baccarat vase of roses, lilies and larkspur atop the enormous Duncan Phyfe table with fourteen-oversized cream chintz covered parsons chairs. She went to the oversized kitchen and adjoining family room. Pam loved to cook and an ample kitchen where the entire family could gather was on the top of her list for their retirement home.

After moving so many times, Pam was at peace in this home. There were no pills stashed in secret hiding places all over the house. She had worked hard to rid herself of the addiction to painkillers. The months after both Rene' and Randolph were shot she needed clarity to take care of everybody. It was her self-appointed job. Her best friend, Anne had recommended a Dr. Kendall to her. He'd treated Anne's sister and she was celebrating six years of sobriety.

The hardest part was telling Randolph. To Pam's surprise, he already knew. He had known for some time and was sure that she would seek help when the time came. He didn't want to shame her and felt she'd confide in him in her own good time. He said he had been planning an intervention but she sought help on her own. At any rate, Dr. Kendall helped her work through a great deal of the pain of her past.

Suppressed trauma is a peculiar thing. You experience physical, psychological or emotional pain and you go on with your life. Often times we think we are just fine, we've forgotten we've forgiven and we've moved on. Dr. Kendall helped Pam realize she'd done none of that. She still saw him once a week and there was no shame in that for her. As a Christian, she'd been taught that prayer was all she needed. As an African American, she'd thought herself too strong for therapy. She'd learned neither of those assertions to be true. Shedding the image of the strong and invincible black woman had given her back her full humanity and an opportunity to heal.

She remembered her mother's awful treatment of her sister, Ella. She saw the disparity even as a small child. She was the favorite and she hated it. It came with its own set of scars. The pain of her mother's death and the way her father had grieved stayed with her. Her father had been her hero, her rock. When her mother Jean died, she saw a rock crumble. It took him a long time to recover and she was worried about him as a young woman; she didn't confront her own terribly convoluted feelings around her mother's death.

Then she reconnected with the incredible hopelessness she felt when Daddy Sloane died. Even now, thoughts of him bring both comfort and tears. She was getting better. She somehow felt he was always with her, helping her, watching over her. His presence was real for Pam. She still had the occasional foreboding vivid dream but she had not taken a pill in over a year and felt healthier than she had in a long time. Slinging her purse over her shoulder, she smiled and grabbed the basket of snacks and headed for the garage to wait for Randolph.

21

Tony Green was a good man. He'd delighted himself in the Lord and had gotten the desires of his heart as the word promised. His heart's desire was Rene'. Tony had loved her since they were teens in Jack and Jill, but he had lost her. He made a mistake countless people make. He was too trusting and too helpful. In trying to help Michelle, he had cast his pearls before swine. He had no idea of the depth of the spirit of envy living within Michelle. It propelled her to set a trap for him just to hurt Rene'. He felt helpless and stupid when it all went down. But he had been patient and faithful and God turned it around. Rene' was his wife. Parker was their son. To God be the glory. He was grateful and happy.

Tony put his cell phone in his sports jacket pocket and went to the nurses' station. He needed to review final charts after making morning rounds. He then prepared to leave for the weekend. He exchanged pleasantries and took the elevator to the basement-parking garage of the Washington Hospital Center. He climbed into the front seat of his aging BMW, the one Rene' teased was about to be an antique classic car.

He felt like he and Rene' had a shot at happiness. They were happy. They both loved Parker. She was able to keep her work in finance going. The sex was good. They were still going on a weekly date and weekend getaways. Church was good. Rene' worked in the church nursery and he was a trustee and on the board of directors for the foundation. They were active and happy. So why was she acting so weird lately. What was going on? Always on her laptop but alone.

Yesterday, she'd gotten up and left the kitchen table with her laptop when he'd come home. She hurriedly greeted him and went upstairs to their bedroom. She was on the phone and terminated the call as soon as he came around. An affair would break him. He knew he wasn't wired that way. He wanted everything to be just fine.

Before starting the car to head over to the Smithsonian, Tony punched in the numbers and waited for Randolph to pick up.

"Hey Tony, we are just getting on I 95 with an estimated arrival time in the city of about one o'clock without any traffic. We are having lunch with Rachel at the Bolling AFB All Hands Club and dropping by to check in on some Navy friends. We will probably eat dinner with them and wait out the rush hour traffic. We should arrive in time to see my boy Parker before bedtime. I won't know about Sunday until we hear from Reagan and Sean. I don't know if they are planning to go out after the christening or have something at the house."

Randolph rattled off his itinerary with the precision of a career military man. These were his troops and they meant the world to him. He'd not given Tony an opportunity to respond.

"Rene's been acting strange lately. She's paranoid at the house and acting a bit secretive. I'm a little worried. Wondered if you knew anything?"

Tony whispered although he was alone in the car.

"No, but I'll ask Pam and then talk to her when we get there. Don't worry Tony. Everything is good."

Tony knew Pam was in the car and privy to at least one side of the conversation. This was not the time to ask further questions so he terminated the call.

"What are you going to ask Pam?" she chimed in as soon as the call was over.

"Tony thinks Rene' has been acting strange these last few months and he's not sure what to make of it. Has she said anything to you?"

"Nothing at all. She's been moody but nothing out of the ordinary." Pam chuckled.

22

Pam's children were a reflection of her. They were complex, thoughtful and creative women. They loved each other deeply and were fiercely protective of all things family. Rachel, the oldest daughter, was the personification of this.

Rachel lounged on the huge grey sofa teaming with yellow and white pillows. Long and lean in her black yoga pants and a bright red Howard University t-shirt, she felt relaxed. Trent would be back from the gym in a little bit. She loved her husband very much and they had gotten beyond his urgency for starting a family. There was a time when she lied constantly about pregnancy tests and where tracking monthly ovulation was the bane of her existence. Those days were over.

She made it clear that she wasn't ready to be anybody's mama, even after they settled on the idea of adopting. She couldn't go through with it. Maybe one day they'd be parents. Maybe never. What was so wrong with not having children? Wasn't the world over populated anyway. She and Trent were the best aunt and uncle Parker and Grace could ask for. They babysat and lavished love, time and gifts on them. For Rachel, right now, that was enough. She had quit her job and started school instead of going through further fertility tests or trying to adopt a child. It was a move that made her happy. She was one year away from completing her PhD in Psychology at Georgetown. Her academic focus was on women, body image and eating disorders.

Things were good. Trent was still working and moving up in his firm. He traveled less and was consequently home more. His need for a baby, a family bigger than just her had not changed. He just stopped talking about it and pressuring her. She knew this need came from some place deep within and she wasn't sure how it was going to play out. His family was cold and unloving and he seemed to want to recreate for his own progeny the parents he wished he'd had.

Lately he wanted all of her time when he was at home. Long walks, playing games, romantic dinners, watching movies or just hanging out. This was exhausting. It was what their marriage was right now and she knew better than to complain. How could she? What was wrong with a husband wanting to spend time with his wife? She'd just have to plow through. Her mom always said, marriage ebbs and flows. She was praying they'd be flowing soon.

Her parents were coming in town and she was excited to see them both. Beyond that excitement came a bit of anxiety as well. They were supposed to meet at the Club at Bolling but she didn't want to. She wasn't as comfortable with her father out in public anymore, especially on base. This was weird because she grew up on navy bases and always felt that a military base was the safest place in the world. The shooting shattered the sense of safety her childhood had given her. She felt no one was safe anywhere. The world was filled with lunatics. Jared was dead but he wasn't the only fool around.

She'd decided they should come to her house for lunch. There was one problem. Her house was a mess. Quitting her job to go to school meant getting rid of the housekeeper to cut costs. It had been her idea. Kind of a preemptive peace offering when pitching the notion of going to school fulltime, which meant intense budget discussions with her money minded husband. It was just the two of them and the three bedroom, three-story townhouse was clean in the technical sense of the word. The two bathrooms were cleaned, the kitchen was clean and there were no dirty dishes in the sink. But their six-year marriage had a rhythm of its own and books and papers cluttered the coffee table, their respective bedside tables and the kitchen counter too. Paper mess was as much a part of their rhythm as pizza and merlot on Friday nights. Trent was always reading something about the latest financial news and she was in a constant state of researching and writing papers. That was who they were together. It was easy and comfortable when Trent wasn't being needy. They were beautiful nerds with no shame to their game until Pamela Sloane Hamilton came to town.

Dad would say nothing but she knew that order was important to him and she wanted him to feel at home in her space. Her mother, on the other hand, was always passive aggressive about these kinds of things. She would bring fresh flowers, place them in a vase and put them on the cluttered table.

Then she'd say, "You know you can't see the flowers on a table if there's a sock on the floor."

This translated to, "You can't even see your lovely furniture with all this crap everywhere. Don't be a pig. Your style does not reflect you, dear"

Rachel walked throughout her house and carefully scooped up the clutter and put it into neat stacks. The stacks were placed on the floor of either her closet or Trent's. The doors closed and voila, she was prepared to meet the approving eyes of her parents for this weekend's christening festivities.

She plopped back onto the couch and called her mother's cell phone.

"Hey mom, how's the traffic?"

"Rachel, what's up lady bug? We're making good time, your dad is driving the speed limit and we should be in the city in about two hours. We will go straight to the club?" Pam was excited whenever she got to spend time with her daughters. She enjoyed every minute. They were funny, smart and kind. Beyond loving them, she liked them.

"That's why I was calling mom, how about you guys come here and have lunch instead." Rachel chided.

"You know I don't care either way, but I know you're busy with school and Trent works so hard all the time, so we just wanted to treat the two of you!" Pam was serious.

"What's wrong? Why the change? What's up?" Pam's questions came in rapid-fire precision.

"Mom, relax. I just don't feel like getting out into traffic. Nothing's wrong. Trent will be home in a bit. He was coming home early today anyway and I thought I'd order something, have it delivered and just enjoy spending some time with you and dad. That's all. I can order anything you want..." Rachel sighed and massaged her temples with her thumb and index finger.

Pam sensed there was more to this but decided to let it go. It wasn't easy for her. With her newfound sobriety, she was a little "extra" as the girls called it and she couldn't help it. He anxiety levels rose quickly. She was working on it and would catch herself more often than not when she was overreacting to something or being too pushy. She was learning psychology terms like self-soothe, self-talk and redirecting.

"Okay hon, sounds fine. Order whatever you guys want. You know your dad will eat anything. So we'll see you in a little bit. Bye."

"Alright, mom. I'm thinking Thai. There's a great new place down the street at DuPont Circle. See you soon, be safe."

Pam pressed the circle on the touch screen and disconnected the call.

23

Randolph needed to stretch his legs. He pulled off the road to an official rest stop and got out to go to the bathroom and walk a bit. He was glad to be retired and to finally have more control of his time.

"Be right back."

"Okay, I'm going to stretch my legs too and put some of this trash out."

Pam went about ridding the car of excess trash. Randolph returned within minutes.

"You okay? Did you have a good little stretch? Feeling better? Do you need me to drive a little bit?"

Pam spoke while munching on cashews, raisins and dates and knowing darn well she didn't want to drive. She asked because it was the right thing to do. She routinely ignored her feelings and did and said what she thought was right, fair or just. It was probably not always a good idea.

Randolph nodded and buckled his seat belt, "Yes ma'am, I'm good to go."

They headed for D.C. with the sounds of Nancy Wilson crooning on about her funny valentine. Neither of them had much to say, each deep in their own thoughts.

Pam spoke first. "So I'm glad Reagan and Sean are finally getting Gracie christened. I'd told her to do it when she was an infant. But she's such a darn renegade that she'd waited and waited and now the babies almost three years old. She should feel embarrassed, little heathen."

Her girls were each so different and she had learned to go with the flow and accept them for who they were and not who she wanted them to be, armed with the knowledge that "all things grow in love."

Pam's mind turned to her youngest daughter. She was piecing together all that Rae did not say and wondering about her behavior these past few months. She was less "preachy" and never had long to talk. Work was always her excuse. She just didn't have time for much of anything. She was too busy. Rae had an apartment off H Street near China Town but she was never home. She'd just said, she might miss them this weekend but she'd try to get back by Sunday morning to make the christening and see everybody.

Her youngest daughter worked hard and brought great passion to her work. Pam was proud of her independence but concerned about her being so distant lately. She leaned back on her headrest and closed her eyes. Randolph reached for her hand. They made their way down the highway listening to the music and watching fall foliage

24

*Reagan was finally happy. This granddaughter of mine was
more loved by God than she could ever know. She had so often felt
condemned because of the choices she made in her youth. Some of
them were awful choices. But God is not capricious and really does
forgive us of our transgressions. Man looks on the outward
appearance, but God sees the heart. Moreover, sometimes those who
look the worst to the world, look the best to God.*

*My only great granddaughter would indeed be christened. I
knew this from the start. Tradition is a funny thing. One often
spends a lifetime running from the teachings of their parents only to
find as they grow in wisdom and age; those same teachings are where
they find the most comfort and safety. Their names were in the book.*

Reagan was giving a lecture tonight and would not see
her parents until Saturday afternoon. They were planning to
take the kids to the zoo on Saturday so she could get things
ready for Grace's christening on Sunday morning. Everyone
would have brunch at their home afterwards. Reagan was
planning fried chicken and waffles, a variety of popovers,
quiche Lorraine, fruit salad and her "family famous" roasted
breakfast potatoes. It was always exciting when the cousins
got together with their grandparents. Rene' and Reagan tried
to get Parker and Grace together for playdates every other
week. Sometimes she'd make the sacrifice to go to church
with them so the kids could play together in the church
nursery on the Sunday's Rene' volunteered. They had a ball
together, always. All hugs and love and it warmed Reagan's

heart to have that with her sister now.

That was usually the only way Reagan could stomach church. She absolutely hated most components of organized religion. She hated the focus on money, the countless offerings and the pomp and circumstance of it all. Reagan was bothered by the casualness of church and the joking and foolishness coming from the pulpit. But what bothered her most was the bullshit lust. From the time she was fourteen, she had been propositioned by good Christian men (mostly married) at church. She learned at an early age how to dodge the lechers and the hugs that went too long. She learned what choirs and choir directors to avoid. It was too much. She could get the same casualness and jokes at sorority meeting, the shake down for money at the mall and the lust ANYWHERE. So she just stayed away unless it was for Parker and Grace to play while she hung out with Rene' or a family worship thing. Sean was okay with it. He did not grow up in church and could take it or leave it. He did believe in God and worked hard to be a good man.

Reagan felt blessed to have him. He was so spiritual and so sexy. Sean was kind and hardworking. He loved Reagan and Grace more than anything else in the world. He had no siblings and was raised by his mother, pretty much by herself. His father left before he started school. His mother died right after they got married and so being a father and having his own family was something Sean needed.

This christening thing was something they both decided to do for Grace despite how they felt about church. It was after a conversation with Rene', Rachel and Rae at lunch. They couldn't get together as often as they wanted to but when they found time, it was never dull.

This time the restaurant was Copeland's at Tyson's Corner.

"So Reagan, when is Grace going to be christened?" Rene' had asked, knowing she was starting something.

"Never." Reagan raised her martini glass in a mock toast to her sisters.

"You aren't serious are you?" Rachel was sincere in her shock.

"I'm down with it! Gracie don't need that bullshit water sprinkled over her!"

Rae blurted it out and was immediately sorry. She took a sip of her Rolling Rock beer and retreated. Rachel put down her fork and pushed her cobb salad away. She took a sip of her sparkling water and then the oldest spoke directly to the youngest.

"Rae! That is sacrilegious. What is wrong with you? Were you christened? Did you grow up in church? Was it bullshit water then? You don't have to agree with everything in church to be a person of faith. You know better than this crazy talk. Damn."

"Okay, maybe bullshit was too strong. Maybe I went too far, but you can't tell me you don't see all the hypocrisy in the church, and it didn't just get there."

Rae spoke while looking down as if concentrating on the okra she was moving around on her vegetable plate.

"Listen, church is not perfect. Nothing is. I don't know why we look for perfection in spiritual places. Christ chose twelve disciples and one of them was a badass backstabbing demon. That doesn't negate the good it does, the tradition and viability of the institution. Damn."

Rene' was calm and continued to eat her pecan pie and sip prosecco from the thin flute. It was her custom to eat dessert first. She said life was too short.

Reagan laughed to the point of embarrassment.

"So Judas was all that? Badass, backstabbing, mofo? Rene' you are too funny. And we cussing hard today I see, so I should punctuate my statement with – damn!"

She banged lightly on the table in mock anger. The table erupted with more laughter. When the laughter died down, Rachel spoke up.

"But you know she's right. You can't throw out the baby with the bath. I know we don't have any children but if we did, I think I'd want to raise them with some kind of spiritual compass"

Rachel defended the cause for christening or baptizing or whatever. Rae was silent but secretly agreed with everything that was said. Reagan made a mental note to talk to Sean some more about it.

"Okay, I'll reconsider it. What could it hurt? Let's get another round of drinks, my treat!"

25

Things are not always what they seem and they that wait on the Lord will renew their strength. They will mount up like eagles, run and not get weary, walk and not faint. Patience is important. Frankie Bea had learned that lesson from his father. Now he was reaping the kindness he had sown. He was a gentle man, a good son and a good friend to have. Frankie Bea was the book you definitely should not judge by the cover.

Frankie Bea wiped the sweat from his brow and laid the rag down on the bathroom counter. Although the house was new, he'd promised his father, Reverend Moses Franklin, that he'd come over and help him get things cleaned up for Miss Ella. He finished wiping down the last of the three bathrooms and prepared to put his rags, brooms, mop, buckets and cleaning supplies in the back of his truck. Walking out through the garage to the driveway where his shiny black Ford F150 sat, he admired the place. The one story brick ranch house was custom made for the happy couple, complete with three-car garage and a huge front porch with rockers and a porch swing. The three-acre lot had a sprawling lawn that he and his dad had created with what seemed like a thousand pallets of sod. And the garden in the back of the house was fenced in and already had raised beds. The front door was white and the shutters were black. It was beautiful in its simplicity. After securing his stuff, he stood propped against his truck taking it all in.

He could not believe the way both of their lives had changed in the last few years. His father was moving into this beautiful five-bedroom home with his new wife. Never having known his mother, who died in childbirth, Frankie had enjoyed the new sense of family he now had. Sunday dinners with his dad and his new stepmother were wonderful. Miss Ella was a good cook and added the warmth of a woman to their gatherings. He saw a side of his dad that he had never seen before. His father was more relaxed, funny and even charming. They still went fishing once a week, sometimes Miss Ella came and sometimes it was just the two of them. But everything was different now, and not just for his dad.

Michelle had been his first love. He loved her since they were small children playing in the dirt. He'd taken her to the junior high school azalea ball and then to the high school prom. Michelle quickly outgrew playing in dirt and being his date. In fact, she outgrew anything that a country boy like him had to offer. She'd gone away to Howard University in Washington, D.C. and he'd done two years at Mississippi Gulf Coast Community College in Gautier and then transferred to the University of South Alabama and majored in business. He thought it would enable him to help his father on the business side of church and help him with his farm and it had served both well. His choice of schools only widened the divide between the two of them. He was a commuter student living at home. He drove the thirty some odd miles one way each day and kept his job he'd had since high school at the pogie plant to make money to buy land. Michelle found everything about that droll and country.

He never gave up and never stopped wanting her. He had hoped she would come around after she saw his little house and the acres of farmland he owned. He'd thought that once she found out how much money he made from farming, she'd change her mind. He was wrong on all counts. After Michelle's car accident, he traveled to Maryland with his father and Miss Ella and realized the life she'd chosen had no place for him. The funny thing was, that once he was there, he saw her differently too. He'd been in love with an image, a ghost, a promise. But he really didn't know this person Michelle had become. After she died, he mourned. But that trip to Maryland changed his life for the better. It shaped his destiny.

Now that he really was in love, he understood. The new woman in his life was amazing. She didn't live in Mississippi but they were together almost every weekend and sometimes more often than that. She was ten years younger than he was and had changed his life in so many ways. For most of his life he'd been a fast food junkie and existed on burgers, fries and fried chicken. When he cooked, it was fried fish or gumbo. But not anymore. She was a runner and a very health conscious gourmet cook. Frankie had lost sixty pounds just jogging with her and sharing delicious home cooked meals they prepared together. She was always going on about a cleanse, a detox and a weekly day of fasting. They'd even done the Daniel Fast together for twenty-one days. This was completely unexpected but it was the most honest, pure relationship he'd ever had. Frankie had a few girlfriends through the years. It was dinners, movies, sex and not a whole lot else. This thing started as friendship and just morphed into something he didn't understand. He wasn't sure where it was going but he was loving every minute of it. Just thinking about her made Frankie Bea chuckle.

He locked up his father's house and left the key under the brand new welcome mat. He wanted to be gone by the time his dad, Miss Ella and the little dog Sheba arrived at their new home followed by the moving van. This was their moment and it was a big one, a good one. He climbed into his truck and headed home. The thirty-minute drive was good for clearing his head. His thoughts turned to her.

26

*Pam and Randolph were not ready for all that was to come,
one rarely is. Nevertheless, there is no escaping your destiny. The
comfort the believer has is knowing that God promised never to leave
or forsake us and HE keeps his promises.*

Randolph turned off the car engine and got out of the
car. He looked around surveying the area as Pam gathered her
purse and locked the door. He climbed the steps and pressed
the button waiting for the buzzer to sound to allow entry.

"Come on in!" Rachel's muffled voice blasted through the
speaker next to the door.

They entered the duplex confronted by two large stately
doors. One was closed and the one on the left was wide open.
Trent emerged in the doorway wearing an olive green V-neck
sweater with brown swede elbow patches and jeans. He was
barefoot. He hugged both of his in-laws and ushered them
inside.

"How was the drive? I hope you guys are hungry. Rachel
has a major feast laid out. What can I get you to drink?" Trent
went on as Rachel approached.

"Hey family! I'm glad you came to the best place first!
You know what's up." Laughing, she hugged Randolph and
Pam and motioned for them to sit down.

"Make yourself comfortable. We're almost ready to eat."

Randolph went to the bathroom to wash up for lunch. Pam followed Rachel into the kitchen.

The house was modern, sleek and beautiful, just like Trent and Rachel. The kitchen had exposed brick walls painted white with a huge center aisle with grey leather bar stools with chrome legs. There was a large wire bowl of lemons in the center of the counter and four yellow plaid placemats. Atop the placemats were oversized white plates and grey, yellow and white paisley cloth napkins held together with silver napkin rings. Pam smiled approvingly and made her way to the kitchen sink to wash her hands.

Rachel had changed into a floor length navy blue cap sleeved cotton dress that drooped off one shoulder. She wore silver Tory Burch sandals. Her permed hair was pulled back into a low ponytail and she wore no makeup. She was beautiful. Pam admired how neat everything was and complimented them on their home. Trent and Rachel accepted the compliment and smiled knowingly at each other.

"Okay, what we have in the Chopped Kitchen today is tom yun goong soup for starters. I know you love shrimp. Next there are two salad choices, steak yam nua and chicken nam sod. Finally, for your entrée, we have a delicious chicken pad thai. As you can see, there are a boatload of spring rolls and wontons, boiled for the health conscious and fried for me. Dinner is served."

Pam and Randolph laughed and took seats. Trent placed three bottles on the table, two uncorked and one sealed. They were bottles of cabernet sauvignon, chardonnay and San Pellegrino. They sat and bowed their heads for a silent grace and dug into the abundance set before them.

"So how's school and work coming along with you two?" Randolph pushed steak in his mouth with the chopsticks.

Trent spoke first. "Everything is fine; we are expanding the firm and moving across the street to a larger office space next month."

Rachel chimed in, "school is so good. It was the best decision I ever made. I really am enjoying the research at the women's clinic and learning so much. I finally feel like I'm making a difference."

They continued to eat and Pam went on about the Pungo Blueberry Festival and the blueberry merlot jam she'd made and brought to them. It was in the car and she'd get it before they left. She talked about traffic, Anne and Jackson, and how Ella Jean and Moses were moving into their new house this weekend. She asked about the last time they saw Gracie or Parker. Chopsticks flew in an orchestrated dance and they ate. Randolph seemed relaxed and it was plain to see that he was enjoying his retirement.

27

"Suffer the little children to come to me and do not forbid them, for the kingdom of heaven is made up of those like them." This is one of the scriptures that comes to mind when I think of my great grandson. The other is, "Greater is he that is in you than he that is in the world." Yes, this is a word for the Green family, especially for little Parker.

Rene' arrived at the museum feeling uneasy and determined not to show it. Parker, thank God, was oblivious to all of it. He lived in a perpetual state of contentment.

"Daddy!" Parker ran across the marble floor and jumped into his squatting daddy's outstretched arms.

"Hey little man," Tony squeezed Parker's baby boy body and looked over his head at his wife Rene's face. She smiled and waved, but her deep brown eyes said everything.

Rene' was frightened. She knew Jared was not dead. She was worried and scared to death for all of them. She worried for her father and Tony because she felt they would be Jared's first targets. She was worried for her mother and sisters because she saw the deep and growing resentment he had for her family. She saw it build up and manifest itself in so many little ways. He started to have to go in and catch up on work during the family's weekly Sunday brunches. Jared made countless excuses to stay away from her family. She was worried for herself and her safety because Jared had left several voice and text messages before the baby was born, telling her he would never live without her. The last threatening message was chilling. Jared begged for her forgiveness before coldly declaring that if she couldn't be happy with him, she wouldn't be happy with anyone. Greater than the fears for the safety of any of those she loved, more than her own safety, she worried for her son. She had come to understand that Jared defined love as ownership. Parker was his son. He loved Parker. He owned Parker. Rene' knew Jared well enough to know that he felt entitled to his son and would destroy anyone who got in the way.

She hugged her husband and they began their walk through the train exhibit guided by Parker's squeals of delight and questions about the trains. They dared not talk about what was on each of their minds for the sake of the boy. Rene' felt if she said too much that she would open a floodgate of tears that would lead to hysteria. Tony feared he would say too much. So they made it through the exhibit, got Parker lunch at the museum restaurant and picked over their salads between bits of small talk and polite conversation. The goal was to beat the rush hour traffic and get back to McLean in time for her parents' visit. They listened to the cheerful sounds of a Gymboree playlist and Parker hummed along holding his new wooden train car as if it was made of pure gold.

"Parker, Grandad and Gigi are coming to see you tonight." Rene' broke the silence.

Parker's whole body shook and he grinned from ear to ear. Each of the three were looking forward to the visit. Parker because they spoiled him mercilessly and he just loved his grandparents, aunts and uncles. Rene', because she knew she would feel better with her mother there. Pam's presence calmed her; it had since she was a little girl. Tony couldn't wait to talk to Randolph more about his concerns. He had been a father figure for him since his dad died and his family had known the Hamilton's for as long as he could remember. Rene' and her father were close. If there was anything he really should be concerned about, Randolph would know.

28

The Lord works in mysterious ways. My youngest granddaughter had a heart of gold. She was fiercely independent and smart like her mother. She reminded me most of the best of Jean, the grandmother she'd never met. There was a brilliance and a spark in Jean that few people saw. Her cruelty was not the core of who she was it was a reaction. It was who she had allowed herself to become. But the Jean I fell in love with, was a lot like my granddaughter, Rae. In another life, born under different circumstances, Jean could have been a totally different person, a better person. I guess that could be said for many of us. Rae was coming to grips with the world and falling in love. She had grown up more in these past three years than anyone in the family really knew. I liked all that I saw. It was predestined and it was good.

Rae stood at the gas stove of the small kitchen stirring the pot bubbling gently in front of her. The aroma of the soup wafted through the kitchen. It was earthy and good. She turned the blue flame down to a simmer and picked vegetables from the basket on the counter. She had picked them from the garden just hours earlier. Now this was organic farm to table. Instinctively, she sang out, *"I'm living my best life…"* and began humming the catchy song. She chose two ripe tomatoes, a head of bib lettuce, a cucumber and a red onion. She held the lettuce underneath the running water before patting it dry and gently breaking off leaves and tossing them into the waiting bowl. She pulled the worn wooden cutting board from the drawer and began slicing the tomatoes and the other vegetables.

She looked down at the worn linoleum floor and around at the white appliances and smiled at the humbleness of the room. No stainless steel here. No granite counter top. No shelves with plants or jars of bright colored decorative vegetables. It was without a theme. No roosters. No Tuscan grapes stenciled on the wall. No courtly checks. No elaborate backsplash. No color scheme. It was a white kitchen with a white floor. Rene' called this kitchen a "bullshit free zone."

She'd recently had planted a small pot of herbs on the windowsill and reached for oregano and basil leaves to mix with avocado oil and balsamic vinegar to make her salad dressing. On the way into town, she had picked up some fresh sourdough bread from one of the farmer's markets run by one of her clients. She had a block of Irish butter sitting on the table softening to room temperature. The bottle of wine was chilling in the fridge and a bottle of champagne was in the freezer to drink with the bowl of berries she'd picked for dessert. She'd gotten crème fraiche to top them. Her mouth watered. This was going to be a feast for the gods.

Eating good food made her happy. Life was too short to eat crap. God had provided this bounty of so many good things and given us taste buds. Rae didn't understand people who ate the same ten things every day.
She sat the plates and utensils on the table in the small dining room and lit some candles, she'd gathered from the back bedroom. There were four matching chairs around the large table. It was old but polished to a shine, with new bamboo placemats she had bought just last month. The room was warm and worn.

From the table you could see the adjoining living room. A huge window, flanked by tan woven curtains, looked out on a spacious lawn and facing the window there was a big brown faux leather couch with no pillows. There was a large wooden coffee table with a book about farming, an almanac and a bible on it. In the corner stood a worn brown lazy boy recliner. The two lamps were large and cheap, but they worked. The television set was not a flat screen. It was not mounted on the wall, but sat on the top of a brown wooden television cart. Covering the floor was a brown and tan outdated shag carpet. It went all through the house except for the kitchen and two bathrooms. It was not chic at all. But she felt more at home here than anywhere else in the world.

The key in the front door turned and the door opened. She could see his shadow and feel the joy of his presence as he made his way to the back of the house. Once in the kitchen he wrapped his arms around her, bending to plant the sweetest kiss on her neck.

"Hey man!" She turned and reached up to place her arms around his neck. They kissed for what seemed like forever. Rae, broke away laughing.

"I can't breathe. Are you trying to kill me?" She squealed in fake distress.

He wiped his mouth with the back of his hand and laughed, "How long you been here? Everything smells so good, the food, the house, you. What's for dinner?"

"I got in this afternoon. So just a few hours. Rented a car from the airport because I knew you'd be busy. I've got all kinds of treats for you; let's start with vegetable soup with some really good bread and a salad. Want a glass of wine?"

He shook his head. "Not yet." Smiling he went to the refrigerator and pulled out a large brown bottle with no label from the top shelf.

"I have something I want you to try."

"I saw it already and I know what it is!" She was almost jumping up and down.

"It's the best batch yet, but I want you to be the judge." He pulled two small glasses from the cabinet over the counter and opened the bottle and poured both of them a drink. She raised her glass and they clinked for a mock toast. The beer was delicious. She'd come to love his small batch craft beers.

"This is so good. It just might be the best yet. Let's sit down in the living room and finish it." She turned the fire off the pot of soup and led him by the hand.

He followed her and admired the petit young woman leading him. Rae was tan with short copper curls close cropped like a boy. At only 22, she looked much younger. She wore khaki shorts and a grey t-shirt that said *Eat Fresh* on it. She was 110 pounds soaking wet. The shirt fit like she'd purchased it in the kids section of the store. It was tight over her small breasts and back and exposed her midriff. The pants were loose and short with cuffs. She wore red flip-flops that cost all of one dollar. The only jewelry was a silver bracelet and a toe ring. He liked the way her tiny hips swayed and decided that following them was a good idea.

They sat on the oversized couch. Rae snuggled close and closed her eyes. The beer with its hints of lime and hops, so cold and so good. Being so close to him was good too. Life was good. She was home.

29

God is not mocked. Whatever a man sows, he's going to reap. I always loved that verse when I was on earth. It made me believe in a higher court of justice. But now, I understand it and see it play out in real time. Translated loosely it means, don't play with God because you get just what you give.

Jared needed to breathe. Kata was suffocating him. His thoughts were suffocating him. He pretended he was asleep until she left the house for the market. He was still while she kissed him and listened as she tiptoed so she wouldn't disturb him. Waiting until the front door closed, he got up to make coffee and start his day. She'd be back soon. She was never gone long.

Kata was a beautiful woman. There was nothing wrong with her except she wasn't Rene'. She had long wavy blond hair and beautiful wide set green eyes. Tall and thin, she laughed easily and moved like a cat. There was mystery to her and he was attracted to that at first. Jared found the way she had pursued him flattering and very attractive.

He'd gone to Valentino Bar, a popular nightspot in Rovini. She worked there as a hostess. He went most nights his first weeks in Croatia. Rovini was a small town off the Adriatic coast that he felt he'd be safe in for a little while. He'd planned on a couple of months and he'd been here over six months now. There had been some setbacks. He needed to be sure no one knew who he was and that the folks looking for him didn't know where he was. At Valentino Bar, there was a crazy custom. The owner would hand out pillows for customers to go and rest on the limestone cliff side. The second week he was there, on a Saturday night, she came to him with pillow in hand, grabbed him by the hand and said, "You're with me." Kata proceeded to lead him to the cliffs. That night, when her shift ended, they sat in silence for hours. As the sun came up, she invited him to her apartment. He was staying in a cheap motel around the corner from the bar and decided her apartment had more creature comforts. That was that.

Within weeks, she was professing her love for this American with the blonde hair and the beautiful eyes. He said his name was Eugene, but that everybody called him Mike. Kata decided that she didn't want to be "everybody" so she called him Michael. They were inseparable. Each using the other to get what they needed for the time being. It was more of a relationship born of convenience and necessity than anything else. Both Jared and Kata were singularly focused.

After what seemed like a sufficient amount of time, Jared decided the coast was clear and got out of bed. Tall and tan in his bare feet and grey drawstring pajama pants, he made his way to the tiny kitchen. He needed coffee. Jared set out to brew a pot of coffee. He poured a cup half-full of whiskey and sat it on the counter. Some people used cream and sugar; he took his coffee with whiskey. He chuckled into the silence. While the coffee was brewing, he moved to his laptop at the small kitchen table and opened it. With a few taps, he was in. There. The kitchen was quiet. Parker's room was quiet too. They hadn't come home from the museum. Jared banged his fist on the table, jumped up to reach for the cup and pour his coffee. He was seething. He was tired of waiting.

Kata would be home soon. He needed to get money to the

guy making his passport and traveling documents. But it was too risky to go out in the daytime. He knew he had been compromised but wasn't sure how just yet. He thought about the last time he had gone to Valentino's to pick Kata up from work and walk her home. A guy followed them to the main road in front of the bar, but didn't come any further. He'd seen him out of the corner of his eyes. So had Kata. Neither of them spoke of it. They walked home in silence.

30

Randolph and Pam had many friends. Moving with the navy every two or three years for thirty years made for a full life with plenty of shipmates. Jackson and Anne were their oldest mutual friends. They'd met when both couples were dating at the Naval Academy. The boys were midshipmen and the girls were young and adventurous. I was still on earth then. It was a lifetime ago.

Making the rounds, they'd had a wonderful lunch with their oldest daughter Rachel and their son-in-law, Trent. Then they dropped in for a short visit to catch up on old times with Admiral Harken and his wife Liz. They had served together twice and been good friends for years. Jay Harkens was a good man and one of only three African American four stars from the Surface Warfare community. He was a genuine guy with a ready smile and quick wit. Finishing up his "twilight" or last tour, he was relaxed and looking forward to life after the navy.

They caught up on old friends: who had retired and who was living where. They made a little more small talk before calling for their wives, who'd disappeared to enjoy a tour of the new home. This was the place they planned to spend their retirement days, or as Jay said, "where they were going to die." He always broke into robust laughter after he said it. Liz and Pam appeared as they prepared to leave. They hugged, said their goodbyes and promised to get together more often because life was too short.

Back in the car, they headed to Tony and Rene's, their final destination for the night.

"You want me to call the kids and tell them we're on the way?" Pam volunteered.

"Sure, tell 'em thirty minutes tops."

Randolph adjusted the ventilation in the car and pulled out of the driveway. They arrived in the sprawling neighborhood peppered with stately Georgian style brick houses with perfectly manicured lawns. They pulled into the well-lit driveway and turned the motor off. All of the exterior lights were on. Motion sensor lights, the tennis court was lit and even the flood lights in the front were shining bright.

Pam's voice interrupted his thoughts. She was standing outside of the car. He hadn't noticed her get out.

"Randolph, come on. Let's get inside."

Tony was standing in the opened doorframe with Parker wrapped around his legs grinning and squealing!

"Gigi! Gigi!" Pam scooped up the little boy and began their reunion talking about the things he loved most. Trains, preschool, train tracks and conductors dominated the conversation. Rene' came to the front of the house and hugged her mom and Parker!

"Group hug!" Rene' screamed as she approached them in white fuzzy bunny slippers, white sweat pants and a pink t-shirt.

Parker loved that and giggled while squeezing both of their necks in his choking hug.

"Let's take your Gigi to her room, Parker."

"What's with all the lights, Tony? Looks like you guys don't pay a light bill." Randolph spoke in jest.

"Talk to my wife. All of a sudden we simulate daytime every night." Tony was serious.

Rene' and Parker walked through the living room and up the front staircase to the guest suite that Pam and Randolph always slept in. Pam took a good look at her daughter. She looked thin and tired.

Rene' wanted desperately to tell her mother what she knew and what she'd been doing for the last six months. She wanted her to know that she had been in contact with Jackson. That Jared was alive and they knew where he was. She wanted her mother to know that she felt scared and unsafe every minute of every day.

"How was lunch with Rachel and Trent? She asked me to participate in her thesis case study on women's health. Did she ask you?"

Rene' rerouted the conversation she wanted to have with a series of questions, knowing that the answers meant little to her.

"Lunch was great, they're doing just fine. No, she didn't ask me, I think she is looking for women in a certain age range and I'm too old. Isn't that right, Parker? Gigi is old!"

Pam laughed while bouncing a giggling Parker on her lap.

Rene' sat on the birds' eye blue sofa across from her mother and Parker. The guest suite had a sitting room, a bathroom and a small kitchenette with a table for two. It was not an in-law suite but it was close to it. Pam was perched on the edge of a sage green club chair with ottoman, bouncing Parker on her knee and tickling him. Parker wore his overalls and bare feet, his body stretching and contorting in delight at his grandmother's touch.

Her gaze was fixed on the blue and green clad king size bed with an array of pillows. The bed her dad called overdressed. He said the bed was too dressed up to sleep in with its' light blue duvet cover donning sage green palm leaves. Randolph teased that the bed was dressed for church or a black tie event. She examined the room as a representation of the life they'd built together. It was good; it was a full and good life. She'd be damned if she was going to lose any of this because of Jared. She could feel her heart racing. The anger was building up.

Tony interrupted her thoughts.

"Randolph and I are going to go for a walk. We'll be back in a minute."

"Okay, see if he's hungry. Mom are you guys hungry? I have a pasta salad in the fridge if you want dinner and some fruit and cheese if you just want something to nibble on. Whatcha feeling like Pamela Hamilton?"

Rene' spoke to both her mom and Tony.

"Rachel and Trent stuffed us to the gills with Thai food. I couldn't eat another thing. Plus I had a glass of wine at Liz and Jay's. But, baby I would love a cup of tea. You got any Earl Grey? Lemons?"

"You know I have your tea Miss Pam. Come on downstairs. I'll put the kettle on."

Mother and daughter headed to the kitchen with Parker, who usually loved walking, content to be perched on his grandmother's hip and carried around the house like a baby. By the time they got downstairs, Tony and Randolph were heading out the door.

"Daddy, did you want something to eat? I can fix you a plate and have it ready for when you get back. Tony and I ate dinner hours ago. Parker has to eat early and unless it's date night, we like to eat with him." Rene' explained.

"I'm good baby. We had a late lunch. I'll get some port or brandy with Tony when we get back, see what his bar is talking about."

Randolph and Tony walked out onto the well-lit sidewalk. Pam sat at the kitchen table and watched as Pam put on the kettle and retrieved the cups and accoutrements for tea. Parker sat on the floor playing busily with his toy basket of mostly trains.

"Want some scones? Shortbread? Lemon bars?"

Rene' pulled boxes from her pantry. Pam shook her head.

"I'm fine, just the tea is good. Come sit down and talk to me."

31

Tony pulled his hood up around his neck and stuffed his hands into the pockets of his Land's End windbreaker. The two men walked in step.

"What's on your mind son?" Randolph spoke first.

"Something's going on and I can't figure it out just yet. Rene' is worried, secretive and jumpy. She's always on guard. Damn, you see all the lights on at my house. The neighbors think we're crazy."

Tony lamented, the worry evident in his tone.

"You know being the mother of a toddler and holding down a consulting business is not easy. There are inherent stresses that women deal with. It could be just that."

Randolph tried to console his son and law. He felt a little out of place because he didn't want to insert himself into the inner workings of their marriage.

"Have you tried talking to her Tony? Did you ask *her* what was wrong?

"Of course I have, many times. I'm like a broken record lately. The answer is always the same. She's fine. Everything is fine. Nothing's wrong. Don't worry."

The night grew colder and Tony wondered if he should mention the call he'd gotten from Rene' this morning before the museum visit. He didn't want her parents to be worried but he thought something was wrong. He blurted out his concerns.

"This morning she thought there was someone in the backyard. A few months ago, we had to pay for installation of a brand new alarm system. When there was nothing wrong with the old one. Rene' is paranoid and I don't know where this is coming from."

"When did you start to notice the changes in behavior, Tony?" Randolph was deep in thought.

"About six months ago and it's gotten progressively worse." Tony confessed.

"Do you think there is something going on psychologically? You're a physician. Any signs of any cognitive issues?"

"Randolph, I'm not an expert in that area, but I don't think so."

With the problems Pam had with addiction, he was wondering if Rene' was taking something. Her erratic behavior could clearly be attributed to drugs. He decided to speak up.

"Well...what about drugs? You think she's on something? I know Pam had a short struggle with painkillers. I know that addiction is hereditary and Jean, Rene's grandmother, struggled with it as well. What do you think?"

Tony struggled to get the words out without offending Randolph

"Listen, I know there is a history of mental illness and a history of addiction. But I don't know. I'll pay attention to her this trip and make sure I talk to her."

Randolph patted the younger man on the back as they walked back towards the house.

"Don't worry. We'll get to the bottom of it."

32

Long ago Joshua sent two spies from the Israeli camp... to cross the river and check out the situation on the other side, especially at Jericho. They arrived at an inn operated by a woman named Rahab. She is an example that the Lord can use anyone.

Kata was glad to be away from Jared. She knew the charade couldn't last much longer. But each day she had to hold on and follow the directions given. She walked to the small house and knocked on the door. The old man moved the curtain at the window slightly. He was expecting her. The door opened. She quickly stepped inside.

"Kata, did anyone see you today? The old man's eyes were kind but piercing.

"No. I wasn't followed today. Jared believes you are my aging uncle. He's checked you out so it doesn't really matter. But I was happier than usual to get here." Kata sighed.

"Everything matters." He spoke softly.

"We have time for some tea. I have everything prepared. Will you share a cup with me?" There is time to talk, time for niceties."

The octogenarian continued. He bowed slightly and left the sparsely furnished room only to emerge within minutes with two ceramic mugs of tea.

"Are you alright? This is not easy work and it is not work meant to be done for long periods of time. Not for as long as I have done it. This is not what I want for you. The end is near and you must be prepared to move on. Have you given thought of what you will do?"

The old man spoke with tenderness.

"I want to go home. I am thinking it is time for me to help take care of my parents and find peace. I have worked many years now to pay off debts that I never owed. I have done things that haunt my memories and bring me waves of shame. But this is the end. He is becoming a mad man, obsessed with his wife and son. She is all he thinks about. He does not sleep. I fear that he is living in a fantasy world and I know his plans are evil."

Kata sipped her tea as she sat across from her frail ally on a rickety and worn wooden chair.

"Are you in love with him?"

She was not expecting this question and remained silent. No answer would come forth.

"I see."

The old man stared silently at a spider crawling on the wall across from the two of them.

"It is time for your call." He spoke softly.

After removing the tea mugs and returning them to his small kitchen, the elderly gentleman ushered her to a windowless room. The room was in the very back of the small house with a chair, a bare table with a cellular phone on tabletop. Kata sat down still stunned by his last question. She knew little of love and had seen men as clients, marks, targets and work for as long as she could remember. She did not have words like friend, lover, covering, husband in her emotional vocabulary. But she knew the answer.

The phone vibrated on cue and she picked it up.

"Yes, I'm here."

The man's voice on the other end spoke with firmness and resolve.

"You know what we need and the end of the week is looking like your deadline. He rattled off a list: The name he will be traveling under. The flight number and carrier if he's flying commercial. If traveling via private plane, I need the full name of the pilot. His cell phone number. Can you get the information?"

"Yes J. M., of course I will."

"Goodbye and be safe. We are ready on this end." Admiral Jackson McDonald hung up the phone.

33

Ella Jean and Moses were in love and they were proof positive
that good things come to those who wait. Moses had raised his son
alone after his wife died in childbirth. He'd been lonely but never
acted on his unfulfilled desires as a man or his loneliness. He'd hired
Ella Jean because she was qualified and needed a job. In being a
blessing, he received a blessing.

The moving van had long since gone and they were
making some progress with their countless boxes. The master
bedroom was set up and sheets were on the bed. The new
bedspread Ella Jean had ordered from the J. C. Penney's
catalogue was still in the plastic bag it came in. She'd put that
on after she got all the dish boxes and pots and pans set up in
the kitchen.

All the furniture they'd bought was in place in the rooms.
Each of them had carefully chosen pieces of their old life to
put into their new home. Moses had brought his old recliner
and Ella had her good dishes and the kitchen table she had
bought on credit when she first moved into the old house.
They had a few empty rooms and looked forward to buying
new furniture to fill them.

Much of the home furnishings from Moses' house was
been donated to people at church when they married. His son
Frankie Bea, or Frank as he liked to be called lately, had taken
the bedroom set and some of his mother's things. But most of
the furniture they moved into their new "forever" home was
from Ella Jean's home she had made for herself and her

deceased daughter, Michelle. These items were the foundation of the new house.

The old house had good memories of their new marriage. It also carried the bad memories of Michelle's defiance and her absence. She had grown ashamed of her mother and her southern roots once she got to Howard University. She wanted to be someone else and her mother's love was no longer enough. Ella spent almost every holiday once Michelle went away to college feeding the homeless with the church or with her sister Pam and her husband Randolph. The old house was a painful reminder of Michelle's rejection. The house also carried the ghost of her mother Jean and the abuse and rejection she suffered at Jean's hands. She was glad the house was no longer her home.

This new home was too good to be true. Her whole life was. Moses was sitting at the kitchen table unpacking a box of pots and pans. Ella was getting them from the table and putting them away in cabinets she had painstakingly placed contact shelf liner on. Moses sipped on a coca cola with salted peanuts in the bottom of the glass bottle. They had stocked the refrigerator the day before. He brought groceries from the local Piggly Wiggly market from a list that Ella had given him while she wiped down the new stainless steel refrigerator. Teamwork. They were becoming a well-oiled machine. Ella wasn't crazy about the new fridge but her sister, Pam, convinced her to get it. She said it would add resale value to the house and look sleek.

First of all, Ella didn't plan to ever sell her house so she didn't need the resale value. Secondly, she didn't give a hoot about "sleek." But she went along with her little sister. Pam had good taste. She couldn't wait for them to come and visit.

"So I thought Frankie would have come to help the moving guys. What happened to him?"

Ella inquired as she stacked a set of dishes neatly into the cabinet.

"You mean Frank don't you? That rascal's new and improved." Moses laughed.

"He said he thought we'd enjoy this more with just the two of us. Came by, cleaned up the bathrooms, the floors, and then left. He called on his way home, said he'd be tied up for a few days. Asked if we needed anything?"

Moses loved his son. But he also knew his son like the back of his hand. He had raised him as a single father just like Ella Jean had Michelle. They were more than father and son. They were friends. He knew something was up but he didn't know what. Whatever it was, he'd determined that it was a good thing. He knew his son would talk to him when he was ready. Frankie Bea was happier than he'd ever seen him.

He had seen some remarkable changes in his son over the past year. He had been chubby all his life. The boy loved to farm and fish, but most of all, he loved to eat. All of a sudden, he was losing weight and calling himself a "pescatarian." Moses had to look it up in the dictionary. He thought the boy was leaving the church. Frankie or Frank as this new cat was called, was dressing better. He had to buy new clothes because the old ones literally fell off him. However, they weren't the kind of clothes Moses was used to seeing him wear. He had dark washed jeans and polo shirts and had taken to wearing suits to church instead of just a dress shirt and pants. He'd started lifting weights.

One Tuesday morning when Moses went to pick him up for their weekly fishing trip, he'd gone inside the house and was shocked by the changes he saw. Everything was neat. There was a weight bench and weights in the room across from the bathroom. There were candles on his coffee table and his dining room table. He'd gone in the kitchen to grab some water and found more candles and plants growing on the windowsill. There was even expensive brown wicker furniture with stripped cushions on the covered back porch. That porch had been empty with the exception of one chair for as long as he could remember. Moses suspected it was the influence of a woman but he never saw him with one and "Frank" never mentioned one.

"My boy done gone GQ on me, Ella." He winked at his wife.

"Well it sure seems that way. If I didn't know better, I'd say Frank was in love. Is he seeing that new girl, Jasmine in the choir? She seems to always find her way to where he is on Sundays." Ella smiled.

"No, I asked him about that girl. He said she wasn't anyone he was interested in. Said it just like that. All cool and smooth. It ain't my business, but I don't want him to get hurt. He sitting on a lotta land and has more money than most people know. Frankie has been working all his life and I don't want anybody setting their sights on him to take all that he's worked to gain."

Moses finished the last of his coke and ate the soggy peanuts.

"Well he'll tell us when he's ready. He's level headed.

Always has been. Nothing like my Michelle. You raised him right honey. "

"Ella Jean, you did the best you could with Michelle. God gives us all free will. You can give your children the best you have and pour every good thing into them and they can still grow up and not meet their full potential. Michelle rejected her upbringing and all that you tried to teach her. Frankie Bea embraced it. That's the only difference."

He got up from his chair and held his wife close to him. Ella Jean let his words play over in her head. She would try to remember them moving forward. At the end of the day, people are responsible for their own choices and reap the crops they sow. It wasn't her fault.

34

Man looks on the outward appearance but God sees the heart. Sometimes the things we think have value and the things we are quick to dismiss and discard turn out to be the most valuable of all. Never judge a book by its cover.

The phone rang. Sean was getting Grace dressed while Reagan cleaned up the breakfast dishes. She was getting more excited than she'd expected about the having her baby christened. Raegan picked up the phone.

"Hey girl, are you guys coming over soon. Mom and Dad up and ready? Grace is about to lose her purple lovin' mind at the idea of seeing her Gigi and Pop-Pop and Parker too! Girl she is about to explode." Both women laughed.

"Tell my baby, auntie Rene' is on her way with Gigi, Parker and the whole crew! Give us a couple of hours. Daddy and Tony went to play a round of golf early this morning. As soon as they are back, we'll head over. Want me to bring anything?

"No, just come on. Bring yourselves. Mom called last night late and gave me a list of things I needed to do to have a successful christening. Hope I don't lose my mind. Get your mother." Reagan joked.

"Girl, you know she wants it done right. You know Pam Sloane. Don't act like you don't. I know everything and everybody had better be in place." Rene' was serious.

She added. "Speaking of everybody being in place, have you heard from that free range Rae Anne Hamilton?"

"That reminds me, I need to call her and see if she's coming home or not." Reagan terminated the call.

Reagan dialed Rae's cell phone number. Rae picked up and sounded as if she was still asleep. It was eleven o'clock.

"Hey, what's up?"

Rae had hesitated and regretted answering the phone as soon as she heard her sister's voice. She just thought something might be wrong because Reagan never called her this early on a Saturday morning.

"What's up with you, baby girl? You one elusive little heifer lately. We can't see you. It's like where in the world is Carmen San Diego?" Reagan teased.

"I'm good. Just busy. What's up? What's so important that I get a call from my big sister at 10:00 in the morning?

"Rae, its 11:00 am on Saturday morning. Are you in D.C.? Are you home? Where are you that it's 10:00?"

Rae dreaded this but knew she had to eventually talk about it. She knew that if anyone could keep her secrets it would be Raegan. Rachel would tell mom and Rene' would tell dad. That was who they were. Raegan, on the other hand, would tell no one. She was a steel trap.

"I'm in Mississippi. I'm going to fly home in the morning to witness baby Grace's pagan ritual." Rae whispered.

"Doing sustainable farm stuff on the weekend? Like a boss! You are on your grind little sister. Are you working with Whole Foods suppliers? What hotel are they putting you up at? What kind of produce is this about?"

Reagan found her sister's work fascinating. She believed that eating clean was important. Both she and Sean agreed that Grace would eat only organic produce and eggs; farm raised chicken, wild caught seafood and very little packaged foods. For the most part, the average Americans' diet was killing them. This was especially true for poor and minority Americans. They often lived in food deserts and did not have access to affordable and healthy produce. Therefore, she was proud that what began as an interest and then a way of life had evolved into a career for Rae.

Rae hesitated. Then blurted her truth out!

"I'm not at a hotel. I'm with a friend, someone I've been dating for about a year now. I'm still in bed. He got up to make a pot of ginseng tea."

"Well, well, well. We are dating are we? That explains why you've been ghost for so long. Who is this mystery man and why haven't we met him? Is it Trevor, the Yale investment banker? Jamal, the personal trainer with all those banging, manly muscles? "

Reagan laughed at her feeble attempt at wit.

"First you have to promise not to tell a living soul."

"Can I tell Sean? I try not to keep stuff from him." Reagan teased her little sister.

"Okay. You can tell Sean but no one else. I'm serious. It's no big deal. I just have to figure it out and wait until the right time to tell everyone. There is so much going on with us all right now."

"Okay. Who is he?"

"Well it's no one you mentioned. He's older and unlike anyone I've ever dated. He's humble, honest, good and unpretentious."

"Stop stalling. Name please?"

"I'd rather not say. I can't, I gotta go. See you tomorrow morning at the church. Bye."

35

Things are seldom exactly as they seem. My mother used to say, "Every goodbye is not gone and every closed eye is not asleep. I'd come to know Jared's mother, Ruth Anne in eternity. She'd never given up her faith even in the midst of addiction, abuse and poverty. It is a dangerous thing to try to determine where folks will spend eternity. There are many "church folk" and preachers of the gospel with Michelle and Jean and many Ruth Anne's in paradise. Faith and forgiveness are the keys.

Jared heard Kata come through the door. He hated how she creeped around so quietly. She moved like a cat.

"Hello Michael, what have you done with the morning?"

Her tone was almost maternal. He hated all things maternal. His mother, Ruth Anne was dead. She'd been a crackhead and Jared saw her trade her body for food and shelter for he and his brother, Joe. He thought of her as a whore, a loser. She was just lost and desperate. She did the best she could. He would never know the horrors she faced as a little girl. Nor would he know the dreams she had for herself and for her sons.

"Just doing some more research on my project."

Jared answered more abruptly than he intended. He lied when they met and said he was in Croatia working on a book. He was an anthropology professor on sabbatical and his

research project had to do with European culture.
She seemed to believe him. She didn't ask any questions and it freed Jared up to be on his laptop most of the time. He was checking on his wife and son. Jared refused to use the term "ex-wife". In his mind, Rene' was and would remain his wife.

Kata went into the bedroom of the small apartment to take off her clothes and emerged wearing a long green embroidered caftan. She stood staring at him for a minute and then made her way into the kitchen to put away the things she'd brought home from the market and to prepare their evening meal. She opened the refrigerator, poured herself a glass of rakija and began slicing bell peppers for the pungena paprika. She had scored fresh octopus and was preparing it for boiling. When it was done, she would chop it up; add tomatoes, olive oil and garlic to make octopus salad. She made it in the late afternoons when she could get the meat fresh so that it could chill for dinner. Kata hummed and moved about her cooking as if she was alone. This suited Jared fine.

His plan was to leave as soon as he got the passports. He was paying a hefty sum for a private jet and a new identity. He would be passing as a corporate executive of a dummy company. This would get him back into the states. Things were going along as planned. Exchanging his American dollars to Croatia's kuna had proven very beneficial to his plans. He felt as if his luck had finally changed. Jared was not blessed. He was lucky or unlucky. He believed in luck, not God.

Jared took advantage of Kata being deep in thought and turned his laptop slightly so that he alone could view the screen. He muted the sound. All morning he watched his son and his beautiful wife. It was bedtime in McLean, Virginia. They were back from the museum and fake Pam was having tea while his boy played. Rene' was more beautiful than ever. He needed them both with him – sooner rather than later. Jared shut the lid down and pushed the computer away from him. Kata looked up.

"Are you okay? Is there something wrong? Is your research becoming more difficult?" She spoke in her characteristic soothing tones.

"No, just problems with the damn Wi-Fi." He lied.

Kata turned her attention back to the octopus, laying out dead, cold and helpless on the wooden cutting board. Chopping firmly and steadily, she wanted to say so much. But the time was not right. Not yet. She wanted to console him for not being able to see his precious wife and son. Poor Jared or "Michael." He was in love. He was obsessed. It gave her small comfort to know; she wasn't the only one in love and obsessed.

36

It is important to remember not to grow weary in doing well. Keep doing the right thing. Sometimes, more often than not, it looks like the bad guys are winning. It may seem as if evil will prevail but wait, be patient. That's why the just have to walk by faith and not by sight.

Jackson picked up the phone and dialed Randolph. They were in D.C. with the kids. He and Anne couldn't make the christening and with all that was going on decided it was prudent not to be there. Rene' agreed that it would be best to avoid each other in the presence of her parents until this was over. They were intuitive enough to catch on. They'd know from the nonverbal communication, the body language, that something was up. Randolph picked up the phone.

"Hey man, what's up?"

"Nothing. Just checking with you. How was last night with the kids? Rene' and Tony doing all right? Everybody good?"

Jackson worked hard to stay loose and sound casual.

"Yeah, we had a good time. Played nine holes with Tony this morning at Westwood in Vienna. It's always good to see that grandson of ours. As a matter of fact, we're headed over to Reagan and Sean's right now. Everything okay with you? Anne and the kids good?"

Randolph rattled off his plan of the day.

"Yep." Jackson hesitated.

"Okay, talk with you later man."

Hanging up Jackson buried his head in his hands.

He wanted to tell Randolph what he knew. He wanted to tell him what he was planning. He had made a promise but was beginning to feel it was not a wise promise to make. He was working with the NCIS. The case had been reopened. But Randolph was his best friend and he valued his input. He needed his input. But he also knew that Randolph had lost the ability to be objective where this subject was concerned. It was extremely personal. He couldn't say anything.

Anne stuck her head in the door of Jackson's home office.

"What time are we going to dinner, Jackson? Are you still up to it?"

"Yes, of course. Reservations are for five o'clock." Jackson was startled by his wife's sudden appearance at the door.

"What you working on and why do you look so strange? Why do you have so many cell phones on your desk? You got girlfriends Jackson? "

Anne entered the room laughing and stood by the door.

The room had mahogany paneling and bookshelves that went from floor to ceiling. It smelled like leather bound books, pipe tobacco and Jackson's cologne. She liked it. It was an important man's room, a decision makers room.
Jackson laughed.

"That's a lot of questions all at once. Let's see. I'm working on a case with NCIS that just came up on someone that worked for me years ago. I look strange because I'm not as beautiful as you, lovely wife. The phones are secured lines for various work related projects. Each one serves its own purpose. And finally, no girlfriends for me. I don't have the money, stamina or inclination. Besides, my wife would kill me."

"You got that right."

Laughing loudly, Anne left the room and went back to the book she was reading.

Jackson wiped all traces of the last conversation clean and locked the phones in his desk. This was something he was going to have to hold on to. Rene' was right. Jared was very much alive and he was headed back to the states planning to be in place within the next thirty days. He was planning to be home for Christmas. Jackson was planning to stop him. This time for good.

37

The family you are born into means something. Don't neglect it or take it for granted. Nurture and protect family. No man is an island.

Gracie twirled in her purple tutu with her hair piled on the top of her head in a beautiful afro puff. She sang her original song loudly as she was composing it on the spot, kinda like improv.

"Gigi is comin' to my house to see me! Parker is comin' to my house to seeee me! Annnnd Pa Pa toooooo!"

Sean looked at his wife and laughed. "She gets that creativity from you."

"Sing baby! Sing! Look at you. Bravo! Bravo!"

Reagan clapped to the delight of the twirling toddler. Indulged and encouraged, Grace bowed and began her B selection. It was another original.

The table was set with hot pinks, turquoise, orange and yellow fiesta ware. There were brightly colored ceramic candleholders and a vase of gerbera daisies in the center of the table. Sean had made a Whole Foods run and picked up stuff to make a solid meal. They'd brought Grace's Little Tikes plastic table out of her bedroom and sat it up next to the main table for she and Parker. Her plastic purple plates with green sippy cups adorned the table. To Grace's delight, Reagan placed a small yellow rose in a miniature bud vase at the center of the table. She put it there for the charm and ambience but made a mental note to move it before Grace or Parker drank the water from the vase.

The doorbell rang and Sean scooped Grace up in his arms to let the family in. Parker bounded through the door and Grace wriggled down from his lap. They hugged and giggled as Sean greeted his father in law with the secret fraternity handshake. His mother in law, Pam came in after him and gave him a hug.

"Come on in, make yourself comfortable. Reagan went upstairs to get dressed." He remained at the door as Tony and Rene' drove up.

Randolph sat down in the living area and swept up Grace to plant kisses and hugs and be in deep conversation with both she and Parker. They were going on about stuff that made sense mostly to them. Randolph was amused and amazed at his progeny. These were his kids' kids and they were beautiful. He felt proud and he felt protective.

Pam kissed Grace and twirled her around in her purple tutu. She told her how fabulous she was and asked where mommy was? Grace pointed to the staircase and mumbled something indecipherable. Pam climbed the stairs to find Reagan. Headed to Reagan and Sean's bedroom, she knocked.

"Hey kiddo, you in here?" Pam waited for a response to enter.

"Come on in mom!" Reagan yelled.

Pam entered the bedroom with shades of turquoise and

brown. They had a huge satin teal headboard with matching turquoise and teal pillows and comforter. There were two brown oversized leather chairs and a treadmill in the room. Large paintings hung on the walls. The art was contemporary and a little confusing for Pam. The walk-in closet was as big as the room itself and had two dressers and two chairs. A small mirror and vanity stood in the corner. Reagan was in a black thong and matching bra in the closet.

"I'm in the closet, come on in and sit down." She called to her mom.

Pam entered the expansive space and kissed her daughter.

"Reagan, I'm so glad the baby is being christened! I'm proud of you baby."

Reagan motioned for her mother to sit down and gave her the glass of champagne she'd been sipping.

"Yes, your heathen daughter, the nonconformist can conform to your social norms from time to time." Reagan teased.

Pam took a sip from the Kate Spade Larabee dot champagne flute and held the stem protectively and with gratitude. She looked straight ahead, almost as if looking past Reagan.

"I thought Rae was the nonconformist. Is she still planning to come in the morning?

"Yes. I just talked to her a few minutes ago. She is dating some mystery man and I think it's serious."

Reagan grabbed a soft pink jumpsuit and sat down on the

chair next to her mother.

"Where are your underwear child? You sit in your chairs with your bare butt like that?" Pam frowned.

"Yes mother, all our chairs have butt juice residue. It's a family tradition." Reagan laughed.

"Not funny. Not cute. Nasty."

Pam was flat in tone.

"So who do you think the guy is?

Reagan was full of curiosity. Pam was silent.

"Does Rene' know? They talk all the time."

Reagan was interrupted by her sister's voice.

"Yes. Rene' knows. But not because Rae told me. I figured it out because I'm a super sleuth and all around bad chick. I figured it out, suspected it all along. Ya gotta watch for the signs!"

Rene' laughed as she stood in the doorway of Reagan and Sean's closet, mimosa in hand.

"So who is it? Is it someone we know? Did they meet up in Mississippi or is it someone who stays there? What part of Mississippi? Your aunt Ella Jean and I know a lot of families in Mississippi"

Pam was amused and curious all at the same time. Before Rene' could answer any of the questions fired at her by her mother and sister. Rachel showed up.

"What the hell are y'all doing in the closet? Why are you acting like this is the club?"

She stood in the doorway, hair pulled back in bun, makeup impeccable. Wearing heeled boots, black pants and a black tunic with a bold silver pendant and matching bracelet, she was visually imposing.

"We are talking about Rae's love life, about to get some great intel. Prior to that, we learned that although Reagan is raising my granddaughter, Gracie as a Christian, she has some filthy ways. Don't sit on her furniture is all I can say."

Pam and Reagan howled!

Rene' looked puzzled about the furniture comment. Rachel kissed her mother and moved inside the closet to join the group of women. Rachel took in the craziness that was the closet. Reagan trying to get her clothes on, Rene' smiling like a Cheshire cat, and Pam laughing mischievously.

"So we R. Kelly now? Trapped in the closet? What in the world?"

Rachel's words served their intended purpose and brought the crowded closet to full-blown laughter.

"No but who is it Rene'? Who is baby girl dating? Tell us what you know."

Reagan wanted to know.

"I ain't telling that girl's business. She will tell you when she wants you to know. However, if you put your thinking caps on and put two and two together, you can figure it out."

Rene' smiled smugly and led the women downstairs to the join the guys and the babies.

38

Rae thought about the house. The master bedroom had a king sized bed with an imposing head and footboard, a blue quilt her boyfriend's mother had made and blue curtains. The dresser was maple, with a high gloss shine. It was huge and way too big for the room. It was nothing like the well-appointed rooms she'd grown up in. Yet, she felt safe and valued in this space.

On the other side of the dining and living rooms, where they had eaten and snuggled last night, there were two additional small bedrooms. One was used for an office with a small desk and desktop computer. The other was a guest room with a full size bed, dresser and chair. The burgundy themed bed in a bag comforter set matched the burgundy curtains. It was basic, comfortable and clean, void of dust and dirt.

The greatest concentration of sustainable farms were in California, Montana, Wisconsin, North Dakota and New York. Although she spent the bulk of her time in these states, the idea was growing traction and popularity in pockets of the south. Rae was really excited about this. At only twenty-two, she was the youngest rep her company had and the only woman of color. She loved working with the black farmers in Alabama, the Carolinas and Mississippi. She felt like she was helping them to discover that the way they had been doing things for ages had been right all along.

Rae sat up naked to drink the cup of tea. Smiling she planted a kiss on the lips of her lover and thanked him.

"You are the absolute best." She smiled.

He slipped under the covers and back into bed wearing his black and white striped Everlane boxers Rae had given him a few months ago. They were an ethical clothing line and he dug it. He'd been living this way all his life. He just didn't know there were fancy names and corporations monetizing the idea of respecting the land and using common sense. The Native Americans had always practiced this and so had his people. To him it was nothing new or innovative. It was just doing right.

"What will your dad say? What will my parents say? What will Aunt Ella say? My sisters?"

She lay close to him on her side staring in his face. The huge man, propped himself up on his elbow.

"My dad wants me to be happy so he will give me his blessing and say it's about time." He chuckled softly.

"Your father will be happy and proud because I am an honest man. I am a man of substance, a man of means, a landowner, a homeowner and an honorable man of good intentions. I ain't tryin' to do wrong by you. I'm tryna do right. Your mother will feel the same. Your sisters love you and want you to be happy. It will be fine. I promise."

"Are you sure we aren't related? We are like those hillbillies you read about, aren't we? Are we cousins, stepbrother and sister, half cousins once removed? We are something, I just can't figure out what. I can't be that. I can't do that."

Rae closed her eyes and opened them again as if she needed to use her sense of sight to help her hear and understand words he had told her many times before.

"We are not cousins. We are not sister and brother, aunt and uncle. We are two people who fell in love."

He was definitive in his words as he kissed her gently.

Rae turned her back to Frankie Bea and placed his large arm around her waist, backing her body into him like a spoon and intertwined her hand in his. She closed her eyes again. This time she whispered to him, herself and the universe.

"Frank B. Franklin, we are in love. We will find a way to tell them."

39

They were closer to the end than they knew. It is because of God's mercy and loving kindness that we are not consumed. His faithfulness is great and there are new mercies each day.

The guys were sitting around discussing politics and sports. Grace and Parker were playing in the middle of the floor. Grace had dumped out what looked like a million Lego Duplo blocks onto the rug.

The Hamilton sisters came down the staircase trailing Reagan. Rene', sandwiched between her two older sisters, was laughing. Rachel joined the babies on the floor and was immediately welcomed into their world of tall towers and toddler construction plans.

"Let's eat guys, everybody come to the table."

Reagan smiled.

"After that the kiddos are off to the zoo and you guys can help me get everything ready for tomorrow. We are putting on the hog because Sean and Reagan can be uptown just like the rest of you bougie folks."

"Sean would you bless the food, honey?"

"I will defer to Rev. Randolph", Sean chided.

Randolph chuckled. His son in law had been teasing him about church and his spirituality for years. He was pretty involved in church; it was a huge part of serving humanity for him. Everyone grabbed hands on cue as a part of a well-rehearsed ritual.

"Bow your heads." Randolph lowered his head and closed his eyes.

"Gracious Lord, thank you for this food that we are about to receive and the nourishment of our bodies, thank you for the hands that prepared it. Bless those less fortunate who do not have food on their tables. Bless every member of this family and build a hedge of protection around each of us. In Jesus name, Amen."

Rene' sat still in guilt and anger, staring at the empty plate in front of her. She wanted to have that "hedge of protection" her father petitioned God about. She also wanted to scream to the entire table to run, duck, strap up or something. Rene' wanted them to know. She had left it all in Jackson and the NCIS's hands. She received periodic updates from Jackson. They were cryptic but they were better than nothing. Jackson promised it would soon be over for good. She didn't know if she could believe that, as much as she wanted to.

Pam and Rachel fixed plates for Grace and Parker, who laughed and giggled at the pleasure of each other's company. The babies were settled and the rest of the crew ate laughing and going on about Rae's love life, the guest list for tomorrow and all that needed to be done.

Pam and Randolph surveyed their children at the brightly adorned table and attempted to enjoy the collaborative feast. They were seated next to each other, each holding a lap full of grandkid. They enjoyed their petit dining experience for all of five minutes and then joined the big table. Grace sat with her granddad eating strawberries from his plate while Parker perched on Pam's lap drinking apple juice from his sippy cup.

Pam thought this family, these babies. Grandchildren were the sweetest part of life. They were so blessed and she was looking forward to Gracie's christening tomorrow and then further down the road, Thanksgiving and Christmas. Parker and Gracie were growing so fast and the kids were settled in to good lives.

"So let's get ready to go to the zoo. Who's with us?"

Randolph asked. He wasn't sure if it was he and Pam or if the others wanted to come along.

"Dad I think you guys got this one. We gonna hang out here and keep these women in check."

Sean laughed along with his brother in laws as he spoke for Tony and Trent.

Gracie and Parker sat anxiously on the bottom step in front of the opened baby gate. Gracie, clad in her purple sweater, purple corduroy pants and her purple high-top sneakers sat smiling next to her cousin. Parker held his train, completely happy in his green field jacket, jeans and train clad socks.

"Say bye-bye guys, we're off to the zoo!"

Pam and Randolph gathered the kids and headed out.

40

Blessed the little children to come to me and do not forbid them, for they really represent the heart of the kingdom of God.

The contemporary church was bright and spacious with sunlight spraying rich colors through the massive stained glass windows. Neat rows of pews divided by a middle aisle held over three hundred people. Only about twenty of them were there for the christening but the way the thing worked, they had to sit for the entire service. The christenings were performed at the end of the service.
They faced the simply eight foot wooden cross and a smooth wooden pulpit with a similar cross on the front of it.

The early service parishioners sat straight backed in their pews. These were the early morning folk. This was the group of churchgoers that were early risers, or conscious of their time. Many of them would play golf after church, brunch, attend a matinee or attend a civic meeting or event. Some had small children and left church for soccer, baseball or football fields. Still others went to work. For sure, these were the people who did not plan to be in church all day. They were less demonstrative, less emotional and most importantly – less interested in being entertained.

On the second row sat Sean, Reagan and Grace. Next to them were Pamela and Randolph, then Parker because the

two grandkids insisted on being next to their grandparents.

Rene' sat between her son and her husband. Tony sat next to his wife. There was room for about six more on their pew. Rachel texted that she would be late but arrived just before the procession began. They had reserved two pews in expectation of two of Sean's cousins who lived in the area, Reagan's friends from work and their families and Grace's godparents. They were friends from college and had driven up from Hampton, Virginia.

Reagan wore an olive green silk dress with pockets and a boat neck while Sean wore a navy blue suit with a striped tie and brown shoes. Little Grace was in white from head to toe. She even had a white bow on her afro puff piled high on the top of her head. It was a grand day and an important one. Dedicating a child to the Lord was an act of fact and a time-honored sacrament. Rae teased that it was basically Mufasa holding up Simba in the Lion King. The gestures were not too far from each other.

The pastor took his place at the pulpit to welcome the congregation.

"Welcome brothers and sisters. This is the day the Lord has made. Let us rejoice and be glad in it. We will do so by singing that great hymn of the church, *Come thy Fount of Every Blessing*. That is hymn number 423 in your hymnal. Let us stand and sing together to the glory of the risen savior."

The choir clad in white robes had just finished the hymn. Everybody sat quietly on their pews. At once down the outside right aisle came Rae, she was late as usual. Rae looked absolutely lovely in soft grey pants with a matching tunic. The girl even wore diamond-studded earrings. She was wearing copper lipstick, grey pumps with a matching clutch purse in one hand. Looking more like an adult woman than anyone in her family had ever seen, she took her place on the end of the pew.

Every adult pair of eyes looked in her direction, both glad to see her and completely surprised. Next to her was Frankie Bea Franklin, Ella Jean's stepson. He wore a tailored dark grey suit and they were holding hands. He smiled, nodded and waved down the pew while Rae looked straight ahead.

"Well I'll be damned."

Rachel whispered.

"And you most certainly will be if you keep cursing in church."

Pam spoke under her breath without looking at any of them.

41

We are taught that the Proverbs were written by King David, providing instruction in prudent behavior, doing what is right and just and fair. It is for giving prudence to those who are simple, knowledge and discretion to the young. Let the wise listen and add to their learning and let the discerning get guidance.

After goodbyes, Randolph and Pam piled into the car. Pam was not sure what to make of Rae and Frank, as he now preferred to be addressed. It had been wonderful to see Rae so happy and they were not blood relatives. She wasn't sure what to feel.

"Well they do have quite a bit in common. They also spent a great deal of time together trying to trace Jared's steps and piece together that nasty business with him and Michelle."

Randolph attempted to make logic of the new couple.

They drove the two and half hours back to Virginia Beach mostly in silence. Pam did not turn on the radio. She did not play music and there were no snacks to issue. They stopped once to use the restroom and once to refuel. They were both tired. It had been a beautiful weekend but they were both exhausted.

The driveway was long and dark but they could see the porch light that Randolph had left on as they passed the large magnolia tree, the pink and white crepe myrtles and approached the two-story farmhouse with six white rocking chairs lined up on the front porch framed by azalea bushes. Randolph pulled the car into the side loading three-car garage and punched the garage door opener on his visor to lower and secure the door. He sat for a moment.

"Home sweet home, Pam."

Getting out of the car, he placed the bags in the mudroom between the garage and the kitchen. Randolph headed to his downstairs office without changing his clothes or unpacking his bags. He closed the door and logged on to his computer. He began the reviewing of old files and data that he'd buried. Something wasn't right. He'd observed Rene' and she was clearly afraid. He knew his daughter. She was looking over her shoulder the whole weekend. Jackson's call was gnawing at him as well. It was less of what he said and more of what he didn't say, or seemed to want to say. Something wasn't right.

Pam got her own bag and took it upstairs. Randolph seemed deep in thought and closed up in his office. She needed to call Ella Jean and Anne. There were two bedrooms downstairs. One was a master suite and the other they were using as an office. Upstairs was another master suite and two additional bedrooms with a shared Jack and Jill bathroom. She thought about how they'd thought long term when they purchased this house and planned to eventually move to the downstairs bedroom and avoid the steps altogether. It should probably happen sooner than later, the suitcase was heavy and the steps felt like Mt. Kilimanjaro.

Pam took a shower and began to unpack. She wanted something to curb the anxiety and the stress she felt. Thankfully, there was no Percocet in her house. She had clawed her way back from full-blown addiction and wasn't about to fall back into that hole again. She shook her head and released "no" into the empty bedroom. Reaching for the phone, she decided to call Anne first.

"Hey, I was debating whether to call you. Jackson won't tell me anything but he's acting weird, when he's home he's in the office with the door closed. Is he talking to Randolph? You okay?"

Anne spoke in hushed tones.

"Yes. We're fine. Gracie was absolutely adorable today and Parker, in his big boy sports jacket and slacks was almost edible. I could gobble both of them up. We're good. I'm tired as I don't know what, but were good."

Pam only partially answered the questions.

"What about Jackson and Randolph? Have they been on the phone all weekend?"

Anne was serious.

"No, Randolph wasn't on the phone a lot at all. He and Tony seemed to be talking about something serious on and off. They think something is going on with Rene'. I don't know."

"Meet me for lunch tomorrow at Lynnhaven Fish House. Let's have a bucket of little neck clams, some wine and figure out what's what." Anne wanted Pam to relax.

"Okay. What time?" Pam whispered.

"How about one o'clock?"

"Okay, I'll be there."

"And Pam? Whatever it is, it will be fine. We can get through this."

"I know. See you tomorrow. I've got news to share about Rae." Pam hung up the phone.

Instead of calling Ella Jean, she called the kids to let them know that they had arrived safely. She wanted to talk to Grace and Parker. She'd missed them both. They were knocked out from all the family fun this weekend. Pam pull back the covers and crawled into bed. Turning off the lamp on her bedside table, she decided sleep was what she needed most. She would talk to her sister about the lovebirds tomorrow.

42

Did I tell you that everything done in the dark will eventually come to the light? I think I did.

Kata made her way to the house for what she felt would be the last time. Things were moving fast. Jared was pretending to be asleep when she left this morning. She had kissed him and quietly exited the small apartment. The morning was brisk as the winds picked up from the west. Kata ducked her head and pulled her thin sweater closed to shield her body from the cool winds.

The door barely opened as the old man beckoned her with his extended and withered hand to come inside. He bolted the door behind her and directed her to sit down. There was a chill in the little house even with the small fire he poked at in the fireplace. There was no time for tea and she was in no mood for small talk. Her head hurt and she felt sick to her stomach.

"Kata, this business is not for everyone. It is not an easy journey. "

He spoke with the wisdom of the ages.

"I know this."

Kata felt defensive.

"When we allow ourselves to lose objectivity, we are compromised. When we are compromised, the mission is compromised. When the mission is compromised, lives are in danger. Even yours."

"What are you saying?"

The pounding in her head grew stronger and louder.

"The spy game is a peculiar one. When you are spying on someone, invariably someone is spying on you too. That is the way it is. That is the way it has always been."

Kata lowered her head and fixed her eyes on her hands clasped in her lap. They did not look like the hands of a thirty-year-old woman. They did not even look familiar. She could not look up at him.

"Go and take your call."

He pointed in the direction of the familiar room, never leaving the flames he stoked.

Jackson knew that it was a matter of time before Randolph would find out. By all indications, he was snooping and had made a few calls. The information was coming slower as time moved on. But there was no time to waste.

"Good morning. Do you have the information?"

"Yes, I do."

Kata took the ink pen in her purse apart and retrieved a tiny slip of paper. She read off the numbers, dates, times and names slowly, as instructed.

"Okay. This is it. Get out of there. Leave before he leaves. Do you understand?"

Jackson was ready to terminate the call.

"There is something else. There is something I must tell you."

She hesitated. The idea of leaving without saying goodbye, the idea of never seeing him again, only made the pounding headache come to a crashing crescendo.

"The house is under surveillance. He watches them every day. The security company installation crew was paid off to not do the job"

Kata felt nothing.

"How long have you known this?"

Jackson was trying to maintain his composure. It was clear to him that she was emotionally involved with Jared.

"Damn it!"

Jackson felt flushed and hot as if his blood was boiling.

"For months."

She hesitated and went on.

"I would be in danger if I said anything. I did not want to anger him. It would have been apparent that I was the one who spoke of it. I was the one in danger. You are not here. It was you, him or me. I chose me. I am telling you now. Be grateful Jackson. Goodbye."

43

Pam woke up to a note from Randolph saying that he'd gone into town to Norfolk to pay Jackson a visit. She decided to linger in bed a little longer before going for her morning walk. She needed to call her sister.

Ella Jean picked up the phone on the first ring. Moses was unpacking boxes in the garage and she was working in one of the guest bedrooms. She still couldn't believe she had all of this space. She felt like she was living lifestyles of the rich and famous.

"Hey Pam, how was your trip? I hated we had to miss it but with moving this weekend, there was no way we could have made it."

"The trip was good. The kids are just fine, but have I got some news for you. Are you sitting down?"

Pam was enjoying the suspense of it all.

"Yes ma'am, I'm sitting down. What in the world is it now? The birds are chirping and the sun is shining. I just finished a good, strong cup of coffee. Don't bring me no bad news."

Ella Jean laughed softly.

"Where was Frankie Bea yesterday? Did he come to church? Have you or Moses heard from him today?"

Pam was serious.

"No, as a matter of fact he wasn't in church yesterday. Now he don't come every Sunday. He's a grown man Pam. We don't be trying to keep no tabs on Frankie. He actually has started going by Frank. But I didn't see him yesterday."

"Well I did. He looked good too. Lost weight, just grinning and everything." Pam teased.

"Where did you see him at? He was in the D.C. area? Why? Doing what?"

"Frank was at Gracie's christening as the guest of Rae Anne Hamilton."

"I know they good friends Pam. They talk a lot and have since the mess with Michelle and Jared. He was always sweet on Michelle and took it really hard. You know Rae has always thought she was a detective. I think they spent time comparing notes and trying to solve the mysteries with who Sheba belonged to and all of that. So did he just come as a friend, like sisters and brothers?"

Ella was confused.

"Do friends hold hands Ella Jean? Girl, they were acting like lovebirds. They were sitting all up on each other and everything!"

"You don't say! "Did you get the chance to talk to her? Did she tell you what was going on?"

Ella chuckled.

Pam explained that she had indeed had time to talk to her youngest daughter when the ceremony was over. She was not surprised by anything Rae did. She had always been unorthodox and Pam admired her for choosing her own path. They'd gone back to Reagan and Sean's and "Frank" had joined them along with the other invited guests. While everyone was downstairs relaxing and socializing after the brunch, Rae asked her mother to join her on the back deck to talk.

Rae explained that it started out as friendship but that they just found that they had so much in common and that they enjoyed spending time together. She said he made her laugh and wasn't arrogant and condescending like the boys she'd known from her private schools and college. He was different in a refreshing and exciting way. She said she thought he was the most authentic and honest man she had ever met. She was in love with him and she wanted her family to be happy for them.

Ella Jean was stunned. She wasn't sure how all this happened right under her nose. How could she have not known? She also wanted to know what Pam thought about the age difference. She wanted to know what Moses thought and if he knew already and just didn't say anything. She promised her sister that she would talk to her husband and get his take. But at the end of the day, both Ella and Pam agreed, if they were happy it was fine with each of them. Finding love is a good thing. Period.

"Well, we are all planning to come to you for Thanksgiving. It will be more exciting than we ever could have imagined. I can't wait."

The sisters said their goodbyes and went on with their day.

44

A good father feels the need to protect his children at his core. It is persistent until his death and perhaps beyond. Randolph is no different in this regard.

The morning had been a difficult one. Jackson had to have a conversation with Rene' that drove her to hysterics. She was inconsolable at the news that Jared had been watching her family. She felt naked, exposed and vulnerable beyond words. Why was this happening? What had she done to deserve this kind of torture?

Anne and Pam were scheduled for lunch today. Anne knew nothing of this. There was nothing she could tell Pam. It was just difficult and it felt like they were going in circles. It felt like something they had sifted through and buried years ago had come back to life. They knew he was coming in on a private jet and they were watching the commercial flights as well. It was a fast moving investigation with lots of surprises. Anne and Pam would have to find out on the back end. The truth was that neither Jackson nor Randolph were foolish enough to think that their wives wouldn't find out. But each man felt that if they did not say the words, they could hold back the floodgates of hysteria for a little while longer.

Jackson briefed NCIS and waited for Randolph to come in. He wasn't sure what he was going to say. He had spoken with Rene' and Tony and they were out of the house. Randolph parked his car and walked to the building, nodding to those he knew as he traveled to Jackson's outer office. Greeting the secretary by name, he was ushered in immediately.

"What's going on Jackson?" Randolph stood at his friend's desk.

"The NCIS reopened Jared's case." Jackson stood as well.

"Why? He's dead."

"New intel proves he is not." Jackson winced.

"Where did you get the new intel?" Randolph countered.

"I can't say, but I do have verification. He's alive and on his way back to the states any day now."

Randolph sat down. He was angry. What did this mean for Rene'? Did she know? He was not going to ask any more questions and he was not leaving Jackson's office until he knew everything that his friend new. Jackson sat down and tapped his fingers on the desk. He felt he had said too much. He did not want to betray Rene's trust but he needed Randolph's help. He did not want to do this without him.

"Talk." Randolph demanded.

45

Rene' hung up the phone after listening to Jackson and ran to Parkers room. She didn't say a word. Snatching her baby up, she ran to the garage, phone and purse in hand. Tony had gone to the hospital. She peeled out of the garage like a NASCAR driver and headed to her Raegan's house. Parker was strapped in the car seat looking sleepy. He was quiet.

Jackson promised that the FBI would sweep the house and the cameras would be destroyed. It would take special equipment and a good bit of time, but it would be done. They were working along with NCIS now. Jared would spend the rest of his life in jail. Rene' called her husband.

"Don't go home. Our house is bugged. Jared has been watching us. Meet me at Reagan's. "

"He's dead. This has to stop. Do we need to move? I gotta get us out of the house. This is bullshit Rene'. It's been three years and now this bitch is watching us? He's in my house?"

Tony was angry; words flew like spit.

"I went to see Jackson months ago Tony. I knew. I just felt it in my spirit. Jackson said. It has been a calamity of errors in judgement and miscalculations. Jared is a survivor. He's well connected and more determined that we ever knew. He feels entitled to me. He's sick. Tony, we never knew him. None of us did, not me, Jackson, dad– not even you. They are closing in. They have a woman and a man watching him and providing intel on a daily basis. He will be captured and locked up before Christmas. Let's just keep calm and not scare the baby. Let's just keep calm."

Rene' spoke in calm whispers watching her child in the rear view mirror. She did not want to upset him.

While driving to meet his wife Tony made a call to their realtor, the one who sold them the house. Tamika was looking for a place for them to rent near Raegan and Sean. He wasn't taking no for an answer, they were getting the hell out of there. He didn't trust what Jared would do next and was through relying on the good Admirals Randolph and Jackson to keep his family safe.

Rene' greeted him as he pulled into the garage and turned off the engine.

"Hold me." She opened his car door and stood in front of him.

"It's going to be fine. I love you."

Tony enveloped Rene' and held her close to him, burying his face into her soft curls. She smelled like honey. He felt powerless to keep his family safe and he hated the feeling. Rene' pulled away with both arms still holding him.

"What's happening? Is Parker safe? Are we safe? Has he been in the house? Does he know where the house is? Does he know where we are at all times?

"We are going to be fine. Let's stay here tonight and

figure things out. I need to know everything you know, Rene'."

He squeezed his wife. She looked sleep deprived and worried. This thing had taken its toll on her and it had to stop.

46

Change is constant and moving forward is better than standing still. Life is continuum.

Tony and Rene' sat in the kitchen drinking coffee from yellow ceramic mugs. Reagan's house was loud, it screamed. Rene' was grateful to Rachel and Trent for coming early to pick the kids up. They were both beyond excited about spending the day with their aunt and uncle. Parker and Grace were unaware of any danger. After organic, cage free scrambled eggs, Ezekiel toast and Reagan's homemade organic apple butter, they were out the door. Rene' actually felt her son was safer away from her and she hated the feeling.

Reagan and Sean had gone for a jog and they were alone in the house. This was their first time alone since Tony got the news from his wife this morning. It was only hours ago but it felt like days. Everything seemed to be moving in slow motion.

"How long have you known?" Tony needed answers.

"Jackson called about an hour after you left for work That's when I found out about the cameras. But I've known for some time that Jared was alive. Why do you keep asking me the same thing over and over again, Tony?"

Rene' spoke cautiously, acutely aware that her husband was

confused and angry.

"Why didn't you tell me?"

"I couldn't and it wouldn't have made a difference."

Rene' didn't know what to feel.

"Listen, Rene'. We are looking at townhouses tomorrow for short-term rental. I'm thinking something furnished for three to six months. Just until the first of the year. Until he's cau…"

Rene' put her fingers to her husband's lips.

"Don't say it. Don't say, until he's caught. I've heard it too many times. We'll move. It's what we have to do."

They finished the coffee as Reagan and Sean were coming into the house. They came to the kitchen and Sean got two bottles of water while Reagan joined her sister and Tony at the table.

"Y'all good?"

She looked at Tony, really referencing her sister's mental state.

"We're good. We gonna look at some temporary places to stay tomorrow. I'm not going in to the hospital for a couple of days. Thanks for letting us hang out here. Just thanks."

Just then, the doorbell rang and Sean went to open it.

"Hey, you!"

Sean hugged Rae and punched her playfully in the shoulder.

He greeted Frank who walked in behind her.

"Surprise! We're back. Frank is staying in town with me for a few days too. Hey man, where is the rest of the tribe?"

Sean points the way with an exaggerated extension of his hand. Rae heads to the kitchen.

"Hey Y'all! So Jared, aka the devil got y'all on the run, all huddled up and what not!"

"Rae!" Reagan gave her sister a stern look of disapproval.

"What?" Too soon? Okay, sorry. Give me some love." She leaned in, kissed each one of them, and then sat on the kitchen counter to lend a ministry of presence. Wearing jeans, boots and a brown and black sweater. Again, she was wearing this new copper lip color. Rae was all aglow.

"We just wanted to be here. They are going to catch him. He can't run forever."

Frank spoke up, "What can we do? Is there anything we can do? Do they know exactly where he is?"

"They know he plans to leave on a private jet within weeks. They know he thinks he owns Parker and me. That's enough." Rene' felt defeated.

47

Victory is not the absence of problems; it is the faith to persevere through the storms and the power in God's presence. Song of Solomon tells us "He does catch the foxes that are ruining the vineyards."

Jared stepped out of the dressing room and admired the way he looked in the black suit. It was a nice fit. The grey shirt and cuff links were not bad either. He was close to the finish line and he felt like a million bucks. Fresh rinse and haircut. Check. Passport. Check. USB Drive. Check. He was smugly smiling at his reflection in the mirror.

He thought about the last few months. What a fool Kata had been. Did she think he didn't know that she was working him? He was no fool. He'd followed her too many times. He'd had her checked out. She had worked on both sides independently and simultaneously. He let her see and know what he wanted to. Because of that, they were expecting him to fly in on a private jet next week. He was leaving today and would be reunited with his family well before the holidays. He was ahead of schedule.

His hair was brown to match the picture on his passport. The dark brown contacts sealed the deal. He was a new man starting all over. He flagged the driver down and made his way to the airport. He just had to remain calm. No luggage, just a briefcase with nothing suspicious in it. As they approached the airport, he paid the driver and stepped up to the curve ready to check in.

Kata arrived at her apartment hoping that she could throw a few things into her purse and make an excuse to leave. But the apartment was empty. There had been a fire. Jared's laptop and his clothes had all been burned. The smell of burning metal and clothing fibers was awful. There was smoke and burning embers in the fireplace. Papers in various stages of damage gave evidence to his madness. They spoke to his meanness and the finality of it all.

In the bedroom, she moved the nightstand and then the rug underneath it. Under the rug was a loose floorboard. She lifted it. The small metal box felt cool in her hands. Sitting on the bed with the box in her hand, she opened it. Kata emptied the contents onto the bed. Stacks of money, passports, birth certificates and identification. She placed most of the items in the inside lining of her purse. Kata took a small needle from the sewing kit in the closet and threaded it. She began sewing the ripped lining in her purse to conceal the stuff from airport security.

Just like that it was done. She walked out into the open air, not thinking about the clothes and personal items left in the apartment. She had done this many times before. This was the last time and she meant it. Jared made promises.

He thought it was over. It wasn't over, not by a long shot. Kata walked to where the drivers were parked and spoke with a man she knew. He agreed to take her to the airport. She didn't know what commercial carrier he took but she knew exactly where he was going.

At the airport, she was careful not to be followed. She went to the ladies room three times. Changed directions twice, sat, and had a cup of coffee. All the faces were different. She did not see anyone lingering and watching. She felt pretty confident that she was safe to travel. Jackson's instructions had been to leave. Stepping up to the ticket counter she smiled at the clerk.

"May I help you?'

The middle-aged woman tried to sound sincere.

"A business class ticket to Dulles International Airport in the United States."

"Round trip or one way ma'am?"

"One way."

Kata counted out the money and took the ticket. She threw her sweater in the trashcan and smoothed out her dress. Her hair was pulled back into a bun at the nape of her neck. She looked severe and imposing. Making her way to her gate, she sat and waited to board the plane.

48

You have heard that it was said, 'Love your neighbor and hate your enemy.' But I tell you, love your enemies and pray for those who persecute you, that you may be sons of your Father in heaven. He causes His sun to rise on the evil and the good, and sends rain on the just and the unjust. It will all be revealed in the end.
Matthew 5:43-45

She could not believe what she was hearing. How could this be? She sat waiting for the airport shuttle to get them to the departing flight area at Reagan International airport. At lunch with Anne the other day, they discussed many things before she received the call from Randolph. Anne wanted to know what was going on. She'd suspected something was up because of her husband's recent mood. When you've lived with someone for over thirty years, you just know.

"What did he say? What's going on? Are you okay?"

Anne put her glass down.

"I'm not okay. I'm a mess and I'm so angry with Randolph. I'm pissed with myself for not seeing through this fool and letting him marry my child and not doing more, knowing more. I am trying not to hate him, feeling a rage that I can't even explain. I trusted the experts. I'm struggling with all of this. Anne, my family is not safe."

Pam was fuming.

"Don't blame yourself and don't change. You are kind and accepting. If you allowed one man to change that, it would be a shame. It is one man. He will be caught. Pam people always show you what they want you to see. They seldom show you who they really are, especially in the beginning."

Anne had been as reassuring as possible. She'd offered to fly to D.C. with her.

Pam, Randolph and Jackson were headed to DC. This time everyone was flying and no one was driving. Pam and Randolph were together. Jackson traveled via military plane with NCIS. Both Jackson and Randolph fully expected to be with the authorities when they apprehended the suspect.

Jackson had cut off ties with Kata but they were still in contact with another informant. This guy was feeding them information on Jared in exchange for leniency. He'd been caught and he was their ace in the hole at this point. As long as he didn't double cross them, this was going to work.

They sat side by side in the blue leather seats. Pam stared out the window. Pam made the decision to not speak with Randolph about any of it. She did not choose to discuss it; she was tired of talking about it. She did not want Randolph distracted and she did not want to say something she would regret. She would get to the bottom of this, when it was over they would have this conversation. She needed answers.

For now, she planned to focus on all that was right. She wanted to lay eyes on Rene', Tony and Parker. To savor the blessing of them being well, alive and having a reasonable portion of strength and good health. She refused to let Jared rob her of another minute with any of her children, but especially with Gracie and Parker. Her grandchildren meant everything to her. She was going to be there. Life was too short.

"I'm sorry."

Randolph spoke as if he had read her mind. Pam reached for his hand and held it. She could not speak.

They landed and took a car to Reagan's where the kids were staying. The house was full.

"Mom!" Rene' ran to her mother when the door opened, squeezing her tightly and fighting back tears.

"It's okay, it's okay. They'll get him this time."

Rae, Reagan and Rachel were all in Reagan's great room. They looked forlorn as if they were at a wake or sitting Shiva. Trent and Sean had gone to work but promised to be close to their phones if anything happened. Tony and Frank were in the kitchen sitting at the table. Pam scanned the room.

"Where are the babies? Where is Parker?"

"Grace is asleep upstairs mom, it's her naptime and she stays on schedule no matter what. She's really excited that Parker's sleeping over for two nights in a row but she was deliriously tired so I put her down."

Reagan spoke up.

"Parker's at preschool because he wanted to go and I didn't want him sitting here listening to all of this crap.

Even when kids don't understand the language, they feel the vibes, the energy. So Reagan dropped him off this morning. They have instructions to release him to Tony, Reagan or me. We are on the list, our signatures are on file. It's fine."

Randolph came into the house on the phone with Jackson. They had just landed at Andrews Air Force Base.

"Plan B. The intel was wrong. He was on to her and fed her incorrect travel plans to get us off his trail. He's here." Jackson whispered.

"Where?" Randolph questioned.

"Headed in the direction of Northern Virginia on interstate 95. Federal agents are headed your way to protect the house and all those in it. Sit tight."

"No. I can't. I'm heading out."

Pam was standing next to her husband.

"Where are you going? Wherever you're going, I'm going too Randolph."

Pam spoke with resolve.

Randolph terminated the call, greeted his daughters and made the announcement he had dreaded.

"Jared is here, in the states, heading this way. The authorities will be here before he gets here. They were dispatched from Quantico at NCIS headquarters and are working with local police as well. Sit tight."

"Parker! Get my baby! Get Parker!"

Rene's scream was one of sheer terror. She and Tony piled in the car and left to drive the fifteen minutes to Parker's, *Little Learners* preschool. Cops were everywhere in unmarked cars. They were followed by two cars.

49

There is a way that seems right to a man, however, the end of that way is death. This biblical truth always reminds me of Jared, but he is not the only one. People want to do what they want to do and often feel they have to make their own rules. They disregard the rules of the universe that are there for all to see. Romans 1:28 predicts their end. And since they did not see fit to acknowledge God, God gave them up to a debased mind to do what ought not to be done.

The woman stood chewing her gum as if her life depended on it. Her hand extended.

"What about the Prada sunglasses? I sent the pictures this morning and you were supposed to have them on. Hell, it's not that damn hard."

Jared scolded.

"I have the sunglasses in my purse, calm down." She put the glasses on. "But I'm gonna need my money first."

Jared handed the woman an envelope filled with crisp one hundred dollar bills. She was the right height and build and she had on one of the outfits in the photographs. Torn jeans and an orange hoodie with a green t-shirt underneath. She wore grey Tom's. Her hair was pulled back in a low ponytail and she was wearing a baseball cap. She was the right shade of caramel.

"Now hurry. Don't mess up or this money will be the

least of your worries."

Jared walked back to his car, wearing the clothes he'd traveled in. Getting through customs was a charm. He'd watched all the NCIS agents staking out areas. He hid in plain sight because nothing about him fit the description of the suspect. Nothing. He felt invincible.

The woman walked through the door and coughed.

"I'm here to get my nephew, Parker Green."

"May I have your name and see your I.D. please?" A small brown woman with long cornrows who was barely out of her teens spoke politely.

The woman pulled the fake drivers' license out of her pocket. Jared had thought of everything. He was thorough if nothing else.

"Can you sign here, I'll go get him."

She pointed at the log. The woman flipped the page and studied the signatures. She duplicated what she saw writing very fast in large loops. Just then, Parker came running out with a picture of a train in his hand. She squatted, outstretched both arms and was careful not to speak. He ran into her arms and she scooped him up and carried him outside to the parking lot. She put him down on the ground and held his hand.

Before Parker could speak, Jared appeared. Jared's palms were sweating and he couldn't believe his eyes. He was looking at his son, in the flesh. Finally, he was face to face with his son. Parker smiled and held his train drawing tightly.

"Hey buddy, what's that? Is that what I think it is? Is that a train? Did you make it?"

Jared was smiling and his questions were rapid fire.

Parker shook his head and held the drawing out with both hands so the man could see it.

"Have you ever been on a real train, Parker?"

"No! Never!" Parker was jumping up and down now.

"You want to go on a real big train and meet a real live conductor."

Jared smiled and reached for the boy.

"Can we go, Aunt Reagan?"

Parker looked to the woman but she was gone.

"Let's go, it will be so much fun. Your mommy will meet us there."

Jared spoke in reassuring tones.

"Will daddy be there too?"

Parker asked, filled with excitement.

"Yes. Definitely." Jared bristled and put the little boy in the car seat, he'd purchased. It was compliance with the law and compliance with the little laws was the best way to not get stopped by local police.

In the car were several toy trains. One wooden two shiny metal ones. Jared handed the wooden Thomas the Tank Engine train to his son.

"This is for you."

Parker squealed a thank you and became totally engrossed with the trains within reach.

Jared slowly left the parking lot and saw the woman pull out behind him. She turned in the opposite direction. He headed for the freeway to the Amtrak at Union Station. Now that he had his son, getting his wife would be a piece of cake. He drove along the highway making sure to obey the speed limit in perfect compliance.

50

A three-stranded chord is not easily broken. Please always remember that.

Randolph and Pam headed to Union Station because they both knew it would be where he would go. It was where the NCIS was making their way to as well. Jackson had telephoned Randolph that they were staking out airports, private airfields, and major train and bus stations. They did not speak to each other during this drive. Randolph talked to Jackson, and Pam silently talked to God.

Rene' and Tony pulled up to Parker's school and ran into the brightly colored foyer. The girl at the desk looked startled. She knew them.

"Hi Dr. and Mrs. Green. Looking for Parker?"

She smiled brightly. Couples like them were her favorites, they made her happy. She called them "relationship goals"; they even had their own hashtag in her inner thoughts.

"Yes, can you get him please? We're in a hurry."

Rene' blurted her words out while pretending to be calm.

"I'm sorry. Your sister just got him. You just missed them. He left with Miss Reagan about ten minutes ago."

Rene' and Tony looked sick. Tony punched in the numbers.

"Reagan, is Parker with you?"
"No, we're all still here. Nothing's changed."

Tony looked at his wife and shook his head. Then he looked at the clerk who was in a state of panic. She grabbed the log and revealed the signature.

"She showed I.D. and signed the log. Was it not your sister, who usually picks him up once a week? She dropped him off this morning too. The same person."

The young woman was desperate.

"What did she look like? Did you see the car they got in? Were they alone?"

"She looked like Miss Reagan. I didn't see her car and when she came in, she was alone. I'm so sorry. Let me get the director, Miss Cheryl."

"That won't be necessary."

Tony and Rene' bolted out of the door and jumped in their car. Not sure where to go and what to do, they called the police first and then Randolph and Pam.

Tony reported their son missing and gave a physical description and details of what he was wearing.

"About 2 ft. 8 inches tall, brown curly hair cut in a high top, close on the sides and back. Hazel eyes and fair olive complexion. He was wearing overalls, a blue and green striped polo shirt with a white color. Over that a green cardigan sweater and on his feet, blue sneakers. He loves trains."

He didn't know why he said the last part. Nothing made sense at this point.

Rene' sat next to him. She was too angry to cry. She could feel what amounted to a lifetime of suppressed anger bubbling up from somewhere she had ignored. She spoke with her mother and then her sisters. Randolph and Tony talked continuously, Randolph relaying a play by play from Jackson and the authorities. They were trying to track the car down.

She went through every moment of her relationship with Jared, beginning with the courtship. He was so sweet and different from any man she had dated. Jared was more confident and more daring. He was fearless. He was everything that she was not. Jared had a way of appearing respectable as if he was lining up with the rules. All the while, he kept a little of himself for himself and did whatever he wanted to do. He did what he could get away with. She had never allowed herself that freedom. Rene' was a "good" girl. She was obedient and compliant. Everything about the relationship felt like rebellion. It was intoxicating.

Jared made her feel special and exotic. He seemed to love the things about her that other men didn't even notice. He thought her curly hair was beautiful. Terms like "nappy" or "kinky" were foreign to him. He just thought it was beautiful and couldn't wrap his head around the idea of perms and relaxers. It was the same with her brown skin. Jared found the hue beautiful and often compared her to the things he loved most, like coffee and dark chocolate and cocoa. It made her feel special and it gave her a sense of freedom that was new.

Rene' remembered being willing to overlook things that had been important to her all her life. Faith, family and fundamental values were skirted with Jared. He would say, "Tell your family we can't make church and brunch; let's stay in bed all day." At first that seemed wonderful. Nevertheless, over time, Rene' didn't want to be deceitful and she didn't want to have to choose between her family and her man.

She watched her sisters and they didn't have to make such choices. She had chosen someone uncomfortable with her world and it was bigger than race. It was ironic because he was a naval officer and fully immersed into the life she had grown up in. However, something was broken in this man. She could not fix it. She felt a pain in her gut as if she had been kicked. "Don't marry potential" was always her mother's warning. Pam would also warn of being unequally yoked with unbelievers. She would say, "Start out like you can hold out, because he's not going to change." Rene' ignored most of this. Now she was paying for it and her baby wasn't safe.

She wanted to kill him for this, for all of it.

51

Kata contemplated what she was about to do. It was not betrayal. It was duty. It was what he deserved for lying to her face and treating her like a pile of trash to be discarded. She sat in the backseat of the car that followed Jared and looked at the words on the screen of her tablet. She paid close attention to the fine print in article 86 of the UCMJ.

§ 765.12 Navy and Marine Corps absentees; rewards.
The following is set forth as it applies to Navy and Marine Corps absentees. The term "absentee," as used in this section, refers to a service member who commits the offense of absence without leave. Cf. article 86 of the Uniform Code of Military Justice (10 U.S.C. 886).

(a)*Payment of rewards -*

(1)*Authority.* When authorized by military officials of the Armed Forces, any civil officer having authority to arrest offenders may apprehend an individual absent without leave from the military service of the United States and deliver him into custody of the military authorities. The receipt of Absentee Wanted by the Armed Forces (DD Form 553) or oral or written notification from military officials or Federal law enforcement officials that the person is absent and that his return to military control is desired is authority for apprehension and will be considered as an offer of a reward. When such a reward has been offered, persons or agency representatives (except salaried officers or employees of the Federal Government, or service members) apprehending or delivering absentees or deserters to military control will be entitled to a payment of

(i) $50 for the apprehension and detention until military authorities assume control, or

(ii) $75 for the apprehension and delivery to military control.

Payment of reward will be made to the person or agency representative actually making the arrest and the turnover or delivery to military control. If two or more persons or agencies join in performing these services, payment may be made jointly or severally but the total payment or payments will not exceed $50 or $75 as applicable. Payment of a reward is authorized whether the absentee or deserter voluntarily surrenders to civil authorities or is apprehended. Payment is not authorized for information merely leading to the apprehension of an absentee or deserter.

(2)*Payment procedure.* The disbursing officer, special disbursing agent or agent officer of the military activity to which an absentee or deserter is first delivered will be responsible for payment of the reward. Payment of rewards will be made on SF 1034 or NAVCOMPT Form 2277 supported by a copy of DD Form 553 or other form or notification that an individual is absent and that his return to military control is desired, and a statement signed by the claimant specifying that he apprehended (or accepted voluntary surrender) and detained the absentee or deserter until military authorities assumed control, or that he apprehended (or accepted voluntary surrender) and delivered the absentee or deserter to military control. If oral notification was made in lieu of written notification, the claimant will so certify and provide the date of notification and the name, rank or rate, title, and organization of the person who made the authorized notice of reward for apprehension of the absentee or deserter.

(b)*Reimbursement for actual expenses -*

(1)*Authority.* When a reward has not been offered or when conditions for payment of a reward otherwise cannot be met, reimbursement, not to exceed $75, may be made to any person or agency for actual expenses incurred in the apprehension and detention or delivery to military control of an absentee or deserter. If two or more persons or agencies join in performing these services, payment may be made jointly or severally, but the total payment or payments may not exceed $25. Reimbursement may not be made for the same apprehension and detention or delivery for which a reward has been paid. Actual expenses for which reimbursement may be made include:

(i) Transportation costs, including mileage at the rate established by the Joint Travel Regulation for travel by privately owned vehicle, for a round trip from either the place of apprehension or civil police headquarters to place of return to military control;

(ii) Meals furnished the service member for which the cost was assumed by the apprehending person or agency representative;

(iii) Telephone or telegraph communication costs;

(iv) Damages to property of the apprehending person or agency if caused directly by the service member during the apprehension, detention, or delivery;

(v) Such other reasonable and necessary expenses incurred in the actual apprehension, detention, or delivery as may be considered justifiable and reimbursable by the commanding officer.

These words were as familiar as an old friend. She had done what she was about to do so many times. Nevertheless, she felt compelled to read the information for the third time, as if she were trying to analyze it. She knew what she was doing. She also knew it had nothing to do with reward money.

Women were constantly pit against one another and even against their better judgment and their best interest, they went along. Jared counted on her caring more about him than herself. He counted on her not caring about Rene', this woman she had never met. Even though he professed love for one and used the other, he felt they were both inconsequential. All that mattered was him. Jared deemed her much too weak and too in love to ever betray him.

Jackson picked up on the first ring.

"Listen carefully. He is driving a grey Buick Regal, Virginia license plate number A62 4418. His hair is brown as are his eyes. He is wearing a very expensive black suit and a grey shirt. He is headed to Union Station. His name is Brett Bennett and he has paperwork to document such. He is carrying two concealed weapons. He has the boy."

Kata hung up the phone and sat back in the car with her head pressed against the seat and her eyes closed. The car stopped within ten minutes. She paid the driver, thanked him politely, got out, and stepped into what looked like a war zone.

52

Jared was five minutes away from the Amtrak station and everything was going according to plan. Sometimes you have to shed the dead weight. At the end of the day, he was starting over and this time was the last time. Kata was a non-issue. His brother Joe was a casualty too. Jared wanted to be free of everyone except Rene' and his son, Jared Jr. He had not seen her yet but he knew when he finally did, they would be fine. She was his wife. This was his son.

Jared looked in the rearview mirror at his son. He was the most beautiful creature he had ever laid eyes on. He was innocent and pure with a decent and loving mother. His life was everything Jared wanted for him, everything he had missed out on. There was one problem: he didn't know his father. Jared had lost precious time in the boy's life. Today was the beginning of changing that forever.

"Hey buddy, can I call you J.J.? Can you say J. J.? It stands for Jared junior. Let's play make believe and pretend that is your new name for today. "

Jared cajoled the little boy.

"I'm Parker. My mommy calls me her boy and my Gigi

calls me pumpkin. But I'm Parker Green. My second name is a color, like Christmas trees. Are we getting close to the trains? I have to go to the bathroom."

Parker was excited to see real trains.

Jared saw the swat team and NSIC vehicles before he parked. There were cars everywhere. He cussed in his head. How had this happened? He would have to turn around. He turned the car to attempt a U-turn and he was blocked. He thought to run, to get out and run. But the boy, he couldn't leave the boy.

Three agents approached the car.

"Sir. Please exit the vehicle."

Two of the men grabbed him and handcuffed his hands behind his back. The third agent motioned to the woman to get the boy out of the car and away from the scene. Pam ran to the car.

"Gigi! I'm going to see a real live train and ride on it! Are you coming too?"

Pam pulled Parker close to her and held him tight. She could not speak, but nodded in affirmation in an attempt to answer his question. Turning away from Jared, she walked towards her car. Parker held on to her and looked at her face.

"Gigi, why are you crying? You don't wanta go on the train? Don't cry."

Parker was confused.

"No Parker. Gigi can't wait to travel with you on the

train. We will go on lots of trips. We can ride the train anytime you want to. I'm crying because I missed you so much and I'm so happy to see you."

She covered his face with kisses.

"Parker, how about we wait in the car for your mommy and daddy. They are on their way. They will be here soon, baby. Then we can decide when we will go see the big trains and ride them. Okay?"

Parker shook his head and smiled.

Jared looked back at his son. By now, he was sitting in the backseat of a regulation vehicle. It was over. In the end, it wasn't the FBI, the Navy Criminal Investigation Services or the police that got him. It was his love for his son and his mistreatment of a woman. He knew Kata was near and he knew she had dropped a dime on him. He knew.

The car door opened. They had taken his weapons, he was vulnerable and trapped. The man got in and sat beside him. Randolph looked straight ahead and spoke softly.

"If I were a lessor man, I would beat the shit out of you right now, handcuffed and all. You do not have your guns. But I still have my gun and I should shoot you in the face and gladly do the time. On the other hand, maybe in the arm, Jared. The way you shot me. However, you are not worth killing. I would hurt two things I love. I love my family with everything in me. My wife, my daughters. We grafted you into something good and whole, despite your brokenness. You shitted on it. You tried to rip us apart. Pitting cousin against cousin, hurting my sister in law, Ella Jean. You broke my little girl, made her cry and lose sleep. You will cry hardest, before it is all over. I love the United States Navy and have dedicated my life to it. Our core values are honor, courage and commitment. You desecrated every bit of that. You are a deserter, a thief."

Jared looked in the opposite direction of this man he once admired, wanting to get away from him. The spirit in him could not stand the scrutiny. He banged on the glass in front of him.

"Get him out of here!"

The uniform cop in the front seat ignored Jared's pleas and got out of the vehicle. Closing the door behind him, he left the father and his ex-son in law alone.

"I need you to know that I will do everything within my power to ensure that they throw the book at you, to make sure you never see the light of day again. Your brother will turn himself in. He's been feeding NCIS intel. He knew you would discard him. He'll take a plea and become a cooperating witness. You will die in Leavenworth. That is my solemn promise. My last bit of advice to you is to stay away from my daughter and my grandson. Stay away from my family. Do not contact them for any reason. If you so much as send a Christmas card, I'll make sure you meet the utmost misfortune in jail. I hope I have made myself clear. "

Randolph got out of the car and went to find his family.

The Future

For I know the plans I have for you," declares the LORD, *"plans to prosper you and not to harm you, plans to give you hope and a future. Then you will call on me, come, and pray to me, and I will listen to you. You will seek me and find me when you seek me with all your heart.*

Jeremiah 29:11-13

53

Sometimes love finds us in the most unusual places. When we open ourselves up to new possibilities and abandon judging people based on their possessions and achievements amazing things happen.

Ella Jean was so excited that the entire family was coming to share Thanksgiving with her and Moses. She couldn't believe it. This is the kind of family Pam had always had and she never thought was even a possibility for her. Now it was her reality. The tides had changed and unspoken prayers were answered.

Frank and Rae had taken to coming over when Rae visited and that was so nice. They played dominoes, put together jigsaw puzzles and sometimes just sat on the front porch, watching the stars and talking. Ella always made her homemade lemonade that Moses loved. But she had also taken to buying La Croix sparkling water and keeping a few cans cold for Rae and Frank. They didn't drink stuff with white sugar in it and that was okay with her. She loved the way Rae's eating habits had rubbed off on Frank. They were good to each other and they were good for each other.

They were making adjustments and learning each other in very new ways. Ella Jean always knew Rae as a niece, a little girl and a precocious teen, but she was now experiencing her as a young woman. She was delightful and full of energy and ideas for living a better life.

Moses confided in her that he had known for some time about their relationship and had given his blessing. He told Frank to be sure he wasn't playing, because that was his wife's blood. He shared with his son that to hurt Ella's niece would be disastrous and have wide-ranging repercussions. Frank assured him that he was serious and that his intentions were honorable. Moses promised his son that he would be his confidant and keep his confidence. He liked the young lady quite a bit.

"So who's sleeping where, Ella? What do you need me to do?"

Moses stood in their new kitchen helping to clear the breakfast dishes. Family was expected to begin arriving tomorrow. Although their little town was growing, there were still not a lot of quality hotels in the area. So most of the family would stay with them and Frank. They'd split them up between the two places. Rachel and Trent were planning to stay with Frank and Rae on the farm.

"Pam and Randolph are with us. All the babies are here. Ain't that sweet Moses, we get little ones under our roof."

Ella chuckled.

"Sheba gone have a fit. He think he the baby. This is going to be fun."

Moses squeezed his wife as they stood at the kitchen sink. The little dog lay peacefully by the back door; he perked up and turned his head their way when he heard his name.

"Sean, Reagan, Grace, Rene', Tony, and Parker are with us as well. We can put Grace and Parker in the back bedroom with the twin beds. I think they'll like that. That will put them across the hall from their mamas and daddies and next door to Pam and Randolph. The sheets are all clean because these are our first overnight guests."

They had friends from church over and some of Moses' relatives had come over for the day from Oceans Springs. But no one had come to stay for five days. That was a long time and it was going to be a grand time.

Ella settled everyone in her mind and started planning her work. She had dusting to do and cleaning the bathrooms, floors and baseboards. The house was never dirty. She liked cleaning. It relaxed her. She had always wanted a big house and a safe place for anyone who needed a place to stay to land. When they first thought about having a home built Moses said five bedrooms were a lot for just two old people. But she had insisted. She was the family matriarch, Pam's big sister. Although, she didn't speak of it often, she always felt it. She wanted to have a place big enough for her little sister and her little sister's family. Now she did.

"So what's on the menu for Thanksgiving, First Lady Franklin?"

Moses continued to dry the coffee cup with the blue dishtowel, rubbing in circular motions.

"Well, we are going to have a feast. I have written everything down. I want to have some of everybody's favorites. We can go grocery shopping this afternoon if you want to."

Ella pulled a yellow pad of lined paper from her kitchen

drawer.

"Moses, are you ready to hear the most delicious Thanksgiving menu in the world written by the most thankful and blessed woman in the world?"

Moses nodded and smiled. He was not accustomed to seeing his wife this way. She was animated and so full of joy. He liked this new enthusiasm. He read her neat cursive writing from the paper.

For Starters

Acorn Squash Soup with Crabmeat (Pam)

Main Course

Smoked Turkey (Frank)
Cornbread Dressing with pork sausage
Ezekiel Bread Sage Oyster stuffing (Rae)
Sweet potato casserole with pecans
Corn pudding
Three Cheese Macaroni and cheese (Pam)
Garlic green beans (Rene')
Brussels Sprouts with bacon (Rachel)
Sautéed Collard Greens with smoked paprika
Yeast Rolls
Irish Honey Butter (Rae)

Desserts
Sweet potato Pie
Pumpkin Chiffon Pie
Pecan Pie
Carrot Cake
Pumpkin Cheesecake (Reagan)

Moses put the pad down on the counter.

"Miss Ella, Miss Ella! That's a lot of good food on that der paper. You gonna mess around and have yourself an annual event!"

He teased his wife and put the last plate in the cupboard. Ella laughed with her whole body and gave her husband a kiss on the cheek. With their breakfast dishes washed, dried and put away, she looked up at the big, smiling red man. With hands on hips, in her most exaggerated southern accent Ella said,

"Let's get us some clothes on and get to shopping."

54

When you seek Him with your whole heart, then you will find Him. This passage speaks of motives and earnest desire. My granddaughter Rae spent a lot of time observing the people around her. She saw those who were truly at peace, those who found joy and those who were simply marking time. She was able to break with traditions and disregard what anyone thought. Only then, did she find freedom and love. She will continue to grow and she and Frank will form a union that will bless many.

After Jared was captured, Rae quit her job and decided to go out on her own. She was doing the same kind of work, assisting farmers to be in compliance with certified organic produce and create sustainable operations. Only now, she was her own boss. Graduate school was still a possibility down the road, but for now, she wanted to grow her business and help Frank with his farm. This meant spending more time with Frank in Mississippi.

This morning, Rae and Frank were making preparations of their own. Little by little, Rae helped Frank transform his home into a warm and inviting space. Rae called it his nest. He looked around at the throw pillows, rugs and black art on the walls. Frank surmised that this must have been what life would have been like growing up with a mother. They say you can't miss what you never had. He found that to be true. He never felt lacking in any way. His father had made a good life for them and he always felt loved and protected. But this.

This thing with Rae was new. It was different. She made his

home and his life better by making the simplest things sweet.

> "So let's put fresh flowers in the bedroom and the
> bathroom that Trent and Rache are going to use. I can pick
> up some from the farmers market when I go into town."

Rae sat with her legs pretzeled in the middle of the big brown
sofa. The scent of jasmine permeated the room from her
homemade candles. She was organizing their preparation on
her iPad. Frank was on the floor doing push-ups wearing only
sweat pants. The muscles on his back were becoming more
and more defined and so was their relationship.

> "That sounds nice." He spoke breathlessly.

> "Let's make omelets with fresh eggs for dinner
> tomorrow night. I'm going to make some fresh soaps with
> lavender and avocado oil. They will love it. This is going to be
> so wonderful, Mr. Franklin. It is going to be the best. They
> arrive tomorrow afternoon. We are going to be ready."

Frank finished his routine and headed for the shower.

> "Make more of the rosemary and coconut oil soap, Rae.
> That one feels so good and it smells good too. I'm going to
> take a quick shower and then clean and polish the floors."

> "Check. I'll make two batches of soap and then head to
> the farmer's market. Why are you taking a shower before you
> do the floors? Do them dirty man."

> Rae called behind Frank laughing. But he was already
in the bathroom by then.

Rae went into the kitchen to prep for her soaps. She poured avocado oil in the pot on the stove and turned the fire down low. She added blocks of glycerin, drops of lavender oil and began to stir with a large wooden spoon. Rae lined six empty tuna cans on the counter and placed a sprig of fresh lavender from the herb pots in each can. She covered the cans with a sheet of waxed paper to set.

The soaps complete, Rae set out to the market. She grabbed her purse and her canvas bag for bringing her things back home.

"I'm gone, Frank. Love you!"

Climbing into Frank's huge truck, Rae headed out. The phone rang.

"Hey baby cakes!" Rachel's voice sang on the other end of the phone.

"Hey, I can't wait for you to get here. Are you all packed?"

"I'm packing now. We are meeting at the airport tomorrow morning at the butt crack of dawn."

Both sisters laughed and Rachel offered flight details.

"We are all flying together, compliments of retired Admiral Randy Hamilton. Dad sprung for all of our tickets. Said it was just a present. He said God had been good to him and he wanted to bless his family. He's the best. Everybody else protested, because they can easily afford to pay for their own flights. Not Trent and Rachel. We are a single income, full-time student household. We said thank you kindly sir and kept it moving! We will arrive around noon and I'll text you flight numbers and all in a few minutes."

Rachel and Rae talked about what clothes to pack for the weather and how formal the small church was and said their goodbyes. "Operation Over the River and Through the Woods to Aunt Ella's House We Go" was in full swing.

55

For this cause a man must leave his mother and father and cleave to his wife, and the two become one flesh. I've said this before, it is important. Man looks on the outward appearance, but God sees the heart.

Randolph sat with his wife eating the crabmeat quiche Pam sat before him moments ago. The salad of fresh field greens, cherry tomatoes and red onions was delicious in its simplicity. Pam sipped her second mimosa and nibbled on the quiche.

"So what did he say? Tell me again, slowly." Pam was serious.

"I've told you twice Pam. He said he was in love with Rae and wanted permission to ask her hand in marriage. Pretty simple. Pretty straight forward."

"So what did you say?" Pam leaned forward.

"I told him yes. I had no problem with them marrying. Do you have an objection? If you do Pam, what is it? Now is the time for honesty. Don't pretend you're good with it to keep the peace with Moses and Ella. Tell the truth woman."

Randolph was firm but enjoying this.

"I am fine with it. They technically are not related. It sounds a little hillbilly but we are not snobs. Bougie yes. Snobs no. Do we like nice things? Yes we sure do. Do we think we're better than anybody else? Absolutely not! Therein lies the difference, Randolph. Most people don't get that. So I am being honest. Besides, I have never seen my baby happier. He has been good for her."

Pam sipped the last of her mimosa and pushed her empty plate away.

"The most important thing to me Pam is that he loves our daughter, is a man of faith and makes an honest living. We just went through a three-year ordeal with a man who had all the bells and whistles. According to the outside world, he was at the top of the food chain. How did that turn out? He is sitting in jail awaiting trial and sentencing.
I think they'll be fine."

Randolph cut another huge slice of the cheesy crab pie sitting in the middle of the table and helped himself to more salad.

"This is good Pam. Thank you." He smiled.

"You are most welcome. If you can't have an intimate brunch with your husband, then what good is an empty nest? I made homemade cinnamon rolls for dessert. More carbs."

She raised her glass in a mock toast.

Pam decided she didn't want to talk about Rae and Frank anymore. She wanted to enjoy this time with her husband. Tonight they would drive to Northern Virginia and stay at Rachel and Trent's to catch an early morning flight. Flying for four hours into Trent Lott International Airport in Moss Point, Mississippi with the whole crew and two sleepy toddlers was going to be hilarious. She sat and savored the time. Pam had not felt this relaxed in years.

Rachel lay the two suitcases on the bed and began placing the neatly folded piles of clothes in the suitcase. She always packed for the both of them. Trent had laid out his clothes the night before. His two ties were draped across the chair next to the bed. She was almost done, but couldn't find his shaving kit. She looked under his sink in the bathroom, then the closet. Rachel decided to save herself the trouble and give him a call. His secretary put her right through.

"Hey, where is your shaving kit? I can't find it."

"It's underneath the sink on your side. I knew you would go in there to get your toiletries and lady things. Bingo. You wouldn't miss it. Yes, I am a sweet husband. Say it."

Trent was grinning.

"You are the sweetest husband I ever had!"

Rachel teased.

"Okay, I got it from here. See you tonight. Remember, mom and dad get here late. They said they would eat something on the road. The spare room has fresh linen and we are good to go. You ready to do this trip, man?"

"It's going to be fun. The oldest Hamilton daughter and the youngest under the same roof should prove for good entertainment. Oil and water or the reserved one and the renegade under one roof. Plus, Frankie's homemade craft beer. Shoot. What's not to like?"

Trent hung up the phone and turned his attention to the spreadsheet on his desk. He went over the numbers for the fifth time. He could not find the error that caused it to kick out of the system. He leaned back in his chair. He was trying to hang on until Rachel finished school. He had talked to his dad and his brother about it. Trent felt a twinge of guilt because he felt he should have talked to his wife before telling anyone. He would find a way to tell her soon that he was going to quit his job.

56

Adeline was with me. It was strange meeting your mother in law beyond the grave. I was blessed to count her as a friend. She rejoiced at the life her daughter's children made for themselves. She saw it come full circle when the prayers were answered. For we know all too well that the effectual fervent prayers of the righteous availeth much.

James 5:16

Parker slept all the way to the airport. He had no idea he would see Gracie and his Gigi within minutes. Rene' looked back at the sweet sleeping little boy. She felt blessed. Blessed that he was alive and with her. He came so close to being another casualty of her poor choices. She couldn't believe she had ever loved Jared and she was so glad she didn't have to see him again. He was gone by the time Tony arrived at Union Station. But Parker was there. She didn't want to think about that day ever again. It was finally over.

"Tony, do you think Frank is too old for Rae? Do you think the family dynamic is kind of weird?

She peered at her husband over the top of her Tori Burch sunglasses.

"Nope."

"I'm serious, Tony. Rae is the smartest of us, she's our

baby. She's a princess. She deserves a king. We've always seen him as Aunt Ella's minister's son. He was awkward and kind of chubby. I don't know Tony. "

Rene' felt a pang of guilt because her feelings and words did not match the Christian principles she claimed to hold dear.

"Look Rene'." Tony pulled into the long-term parking lot at Dulles airport.

"This is how I see it. Because Rae is smart, she knows what she wants. I've watch your sister look past so much bullshit from guys who thought she was a young tenderoni redbone with 'good' hair. She kicked them to the curb with a quickness. This dude sees her as a person. They seem to have a lot in common and to bring out the best in each other."

Rene' was nodding.

"Finally babe, how do you know he's not a prince?"

Tony winked at his wife and turned off the car engine.

Rene' grabbed Tony's hand, brought it to her lips and kissed the back of his hand.

"Thank you." She whispered.

"You're welcome. But what am I being thanked for?"

"Thanks for loving me, for loving another man's son as your own. Thank you for standing by me through all the craziness of the past few years. Thank you for being wise and kind. Did I say thanks for loving me?"

"Rene', I've loved you since we were in the fourth

grade and you beat my time on the Rubik's cube without breaking a sweat. I fell in love when we were playing monopoly together when our families visited one another. I think it was love at first sight. I told my little brother years ago that you were the smartest, prettiest girl I'd ever seen. You still are. "

Tony was serious.

By the time they got to the gate, the whole family was there. Parker was awake and groggy but alert enough to play with Grace and squeal about being in the presence of his Gigi and Pa-Pa. The two toddlers were absorbed by Pam and Randolph at one end of a long row of seats at the gate.

Reagan and Sean sat sipping Starbucks coffee, trying to wake up. She watched the kids play and still could not get over the fact that Jared had used her likeness and her name in his attempt to steal Parker away from their family. She was angry. No matter how many times Rene', Rachel and her mom said to let it go; she was having a hard time doing so. Sean spoke to her quietly.

"What's on your mind?"

"Nothing. Seeing Parker makes me want to fight Jared. I mean WWF style."

"Let it go."

Sean squeezed his wife's thigh and smiled. Reagan sighed. This was a happy time. Rachel alternated her holidays between Trent's family and her own. This year she would spend Christmas with Trent's family in Palm Beach and her family would get both she and Trent for Thanksgiving.

Reagan knew she shouldn't waste this time with regret and Jared's negativity. She would indeed try to let it go.

57

Now these three remain: Faith, hope and love. The greatest of these is love. Always.

Waking up in Frank's house, Rachel felt relaxed. It was serene and quiet. Rae had made amazing omelets for dinner with homemade spelt biscuits and honey butter. They had fresh green beans from their garden and they tasted better than any green beans she had ever tasted. Rachel had never seen Trent eat so much. It was all so good. After dinner, they had adjourned to the living room and enjoyed homemade brew. They drank beer after beer until relaxation turned to drowsiness. Finally, she and Trent had taken a shower together with the most heavenly handmade herbal soap. They made love; fell into a deep and comfortable sleep.

"Wake up sleepy head. Happy Turkey Day in Mississippi."

Rachel spooned her naked husband, with her breast pressed against his back, she whispered in his ear.

"Good morning. Why are you on me like this early in the morning? It's a holiday, Rachel. I'm not some boy toy you can just use."

Trent was jovial and teasing.

"Boy ain't nobody on you like that this morning."

Rachel pinched his butt and lay flat on her back. Trent turned around to face her. He smiled and patted her stomach on top of the organic cotton duvet.

"Trent, this seems like such a good life. Do you know we are going out to gather fresh eggs this morning? Rae is squeezing fresh orange juice as we speak. Fresh everything and not at the prices we pay. Oh my God! It is so good. No people. No neighbors near. No city noises. No traffic."

"Rachel, it is miles away from our hectic life and my grueling job. Sometimes I feel like I'm the middle rat in the rat race. But it's also miles away from galleries, restaurants and some of the things I think we love. Baby, let's not over think it, let's just enjoy these five days."

They lay there, each contemplating change and taking stock of the life they had built and the direction, they were going in. Her sister's knock on the door disrupted their thoughts.

"Hey sleepy heads. They want us over at aunt Ella's by three. Can I come in? Y'all decent?"

"Come on in. We're booty butt naked but you're an open minded liberal?"

Rachel laughed at her newfound boldness. Trent poked her side in disapproval.

"Girl, get dressed and let's gather these eggs. I am Pamela Sloane Hamilton's daughter. I ain't never gonna get that liberal. Listen, Aunt Ella wants you to make brussels sprouts with bacon. I picked up the sprouts from the farmer's market yesterday. Let's get going."

They laughed and got up to begin this holiday. Trent showered and went to find Frank out back smoking the turkey after his wife joined her sister at the chicken coop.

The sisters stood side by side in the hen house gathering eggs. Their rubber boots and sweaters made for a beautiful fall picture. Rachel marveled at how the air smelled so good, so clean. Granted, the chicken coop didn't smell so great but the fresh morning outside was priceless.

They all met up in the kitchen for leftover biscuits and Pam's homemade mixed berry jam made from Pungo, Virginia blueberries and strawberries. The four of them shared a huge pot of coffee. The small kitchen was warm and inviting. Trent asked questions about sustainable farming and what kind of crops could grow in Mississippi soil. They talked agriculture and horticulture. Trent had a secret desire in his heart that only his Creator new about.

Rachel got up from the table to cut the brussels sprouts in half and prep them for cooking. She set aside two cups of sprouts to cook without the bacon, just for her baby sister. Rae sat watching her big sister slice bacon and cut brussels sprouts in half. She talked to Rachel and Trent about their idea to create an organic market co-op. This would be different from the farmer's market. All the merchants would have certified organic produce. There were many older farmers with small gardens who could benefit from the income. They were locked out of the traditional sales outlets and most of them didn't even know they qualified. They simply grew things the way they had always done. There was simplicity and honesty in their harvest. She wanted to harness their efforts and their expertise and share it with this new generation living off fast food alon

58

The first shall be last and the last shall be first. If you are able to stay humble and to do what is just, in due time you will get your reward.

Ella Jean sat rocking on the front porch with her sister. The morning was cool as they watched Grace and Parker run in circles in the front yard playing with two neon-inflated balls. They rolled them, bounced on them and tried to toss them. The toys were a welcome gift from their great Aunt Ella and Uncle Moses. Always resourceful, she had thought of everything.

Pam sipped her Earl Grey tea while Ella drank her usual hot water and lemon. She had it most mornings before coffee or breakfast. They didn't mind the brisk November weather. It felt warm.

"How'd we get here? Who would have thought it?" Pam spoke first.

"By the grace of God, child." Ella Jean whispered. She continued.

"We've been through so much and we standing. They say that which doesn't kill you, only makes you stronger. We survived and thrived."

"Our families are healthy and whole and are about to be blended in the craziest way. This Rae and Frank thing." Pam took another sip of tea.

"How you feelin' bout all of dat, sister? He ain't like Trent, Tony and Sean. No fancy college or Jacks and Jills and all that. State school minister's son. Frankie Bea is a country boy. Dat don't bother you none?"

Ella put her cup on the little white table between them and looked directly at her sister.

"Ella Jean, I tried to raise the girls as individuals. Tried to do better than Mama did by us. I searched for their strengths and weaknesses and tried to nurture both, encourage their passions and interests. Let them be. Rae is not her sisters. Rae is Rae. He makes her happy and that makes me happy. I struggled with it for a second. But I am good."

Pam punctuated her conversation with a sip of tea and continued to talk.

"Frank is a fine man. He's honest and knows the Lord. He makes a good living, probably has a greater net worth than some of the others." She laughed.

"Besides, the woman that helped raise him is the same woman that helped raise me. You."

"My God, I wish Daddy Sloane was here to see what we made of the life he tried to build for us."

Ella fought back the tears. They were tears of joy.

Parker and Grace interrupted just as the two sisters sat reminiscing about growing up, laughing about the good times and trying to making sense of the bad times. The babies wanted to go inside and play with Sheba. Pam needed to start her macaroni and cheese anyway. They were expecting Rachel and Rae soon.

Rene' and Reagan were preparing dishes while the guys watched football in the family room. They each had nutcrackers and a small bowl of nuts taken from the large bowl on the coffee table. They kept their hands busy with an assortment of walnuts, pecans and hazel nuts. Sipping on homemade ice tea, Tony and Sean had quietly spiked theirs with Jack Daniels. Moses was proud of his 90" plasma wall mounted flat screen. He told the group last night that it was the biggest TV he had ever seen and they were going to feel like they were on the fifty-yard line when they watched the game.

Pam got the kids settled. The house became a blur of motion. Rae and Rachel arrived with their assigned dishes and began ironing tablecloths and setting the table. Pam and Ella cooked and kept a keen eye on all that was going on. This was Ella's first big holiday dinner and she was thankful for her double ovens. She couldn't believe how much time they saved. The stainless steel was growing on her too.

By the time they changed clothes and sat down, they were a Mahogany Hallmark card. Beautiful, happy and blessed. Moses prayed the blessing.

Dear Lord in heaven, make us truly thankful for this our bounty. Bless the loving hands that prepared this meal and make it good for the nourishment of our body and the fellowship good for the nourishment of our souls. Thank you for your manifold blessings this day, for truly our souls look back and wonder how we got over.

But for your grace. In Jesus name. Amen.

Ella and Moses had purchased two plastic booster seats so that the parents could travel light. They felt mighty big as they sat side by side flanked by their Gigi and Pa-Pa. Moses asked everyone to say something they were thankful for after grace. Grace and Parker were prompted by Pam and said the same thing.

"Mommy and Daddy."

Frank went last and got up from the table. He pulled a black velvet box from somewhere and knelt in front of Rae.

"I am Thankful for Miss Ella marrying my father and for finally having a family. I am thankful for favor and prosperity that I have done nothing to deserve. But most of all, I am thankful for this woman."

Removing the rose gold ring with a large topaz stone from the box, he looked directly at Rae, who was crying.

"Rae, you have made me happier than I thought possible. You have changed my life and I can't imagine living the rest of it without you. Will you marry me?"

The small woman jumped up from the chair and embraced Frank.

"Yes. It is all I want. Yes, man. Yes!"

Epilogue

I told you the story because I promised you that I would. My daughters, Pamela and Ella Jean's, love will continue to thrive. They will enjoy this Thanksgiving, as it is a predestined turning point. Every life has times, places and people that literally and purposefully redirect their lives. Because "whom he foreknew he predestined." They will all join me and I will be here waiting for all eternity.

Pam and Randolph have plans for everyone to meet at their home for Christmas, not everyone will be there. Rachel will share the holiday with Trent's family. All the others will be there. Pam will create a family feast to remember. Ella Jean will sleep at her sister's house as a married woman and attend their church as a married woman and a first lady. These firsts will build her confidence and faith. He is indeed the potter and we are the clay. In the twinkling of an eye, things can change. Love will permeate their time together and they will make memories that will last a lifetime.

Rae and Frank will marry and become the first African American millionaires in the organic food industry with their own label and brand. They will even grace the cover of Forbes magazine. Eventually, they are the largest landowners in the county and they break down many barriers to reach those milestones. The four Franklin children will rise up and bless them with their discipline, their talent and their love. They will have three sons and finally a daughter. Abundant life is theirs to have.

Trent has a deep desire to quit his job and start a winery. Frank was the catalyst the Lord used to motivate and lead him to his destiny. He and Rachel will struggle with the idea. However, eventually they move to Mississippi and his dream takes seed. They expand to California and just make beautiful wines. Their faith flourishes and is strengthened. Reading about two children, seven and ten, orphaned in a fire, Rachel will feel something new. Moved by the Holy Spirit, she and Trent adopt Brian and Bella. These children are a part of their destiny and give each of them something they were lacking.

Though they do not know it yet, Reagan is pregnant with Gracie's little sister. The word says in this world, you will have tribulations, but be of good cheer. They will have their share of obstacles but know that they will overcome them all. Reaping good seed brings a good harvest.

Pam and Ella will remain close until the day they die. Pam will depart this earth years before her sister and Ella will serve as the mother figure to the entire clan once she is gone. They will grieve, but they will endure. In leaving, Pam will unknowingly bequeath her sister replacement daughters to love. Such are the ties that bind. Randolph will join us in eternity one year after his wife. He will literally will himself to die. Many will say, he died of a broken heart but I can tell you his time, date and place were in the book the day he was born. It is that way for all of us.

Tony and Rene' will only have the one child, Parker. He will make his mark on the world in a most unexpected way. There is so much goodness to come. You wonder most about Jared, Joe and Kata. I will not waste much time on them for they do not belong to me. They are neither my progeny or of this world. They will die as all men do. Jared dies as he lived, by the sword. It will not be long before he joins my wife Jean and Michelle.

If you are wondering why the past and the future were the shortest part of my story, know that there is a reason. The past is vital for learning who you are and where you have come from. It will guide you if you are wise. However, we must not dwell on it, *for it will rob you of the present and you're your future. The future is not promised to us but it is intricately tethered to the present. What we build today is what we will have tomorrow. But don't spend too much time in the future. Many people live by "I can't wait until..." This is unwise.*

The present is now. This is what you have. This is always where we should live. This is the largest part of each life. It is where our focus must be. My advice is to live each day as if it were your last. Seek first the important things, the kingdom of God and His righteousness and all the other things will come.

I have watched and prayed. But I am not alone. There are those here with me who watch over those they love on earth just as I do. The body dies. Ashes to ashes, dust to dust, but love never dies. We are watching, celebrating your victories and rejoicing along with you. You would be wise to know that you are not alone. You are loved and even in darkness there is a guiding light.

*"By day the LORD went ahead of them in a pillar of cloud to guide them on their way and by night in **a pillar of fire** to give them light, so that they could travel by day or night."*
Exodus 13:21

~ Jonas Ezra Sloane

ABOUT THE AUTHOR

Casey Curry is the director of an award winning creative writing program at a fine arts magnet school in Tampa, Florida. She is a writing coach and facilitates local and national writing workshops. Casey believes that everyone has a story and every story has value and as such, she is passionate and relentless in her support of emerging writers. The mother of four daughters, Casey spends her time writing, cooking, entertaining with her husband and most of all enjoying their empty nest.

51434575R00140

Made in the USA
Columbia, SC
22 February 2019